I0822674

Bounty: Wanted Dead or Alive

Direwolf Bounty Hunter Agency

Adalynd Grayves

Copyright © 2023 Adalynd Grayves

All rights reserved.

No part of this publication may be reproduced, distributed, or transmitted in any form or by any means, including photocopying, recording, or other electronic or mechanical methods, without the prior written permission of the publisher, except as permitted by U.S. copyright law. For permission requests, contact Wanderlust Ink Press/ Adalynd Grayves.

The story, all names, characters, and incidents portrayed in this production are fictitious. No identification with actual persons (living or deceased), places, buildings, and products is intended or should be inferred.

Book Cover by Wanderlust Ink & Tome

Chapter Headers & Scene Breaks by Enchanting Designs by Tocilj

Editing by Red Umbrella

Copyedits by Inessa Sage

www.adalyndgrayves.com

For Rachael

Before You Read

Bounty takes place in a fictional setting in our own world. Time placement would be early 2000s. There are some dudes, f-bombs, and darker imagery within the book. If this is not your cuppa I understand. Want to dive in anyway? Always check my site for the content descriptions before continuing.

DIREWOLF BOUNTY HUNTER AGENCY

From left to right Fenris and Aaima in front, with Abraxas and Stephen in back.

Contents

Chapter One

First Day Back

Aaima

Dread filled every fiber of my being, paralyzing me outside the entrance of the DBA office. It took everything I had to keep from turning back as I relived the last night I spent with my dad. Our final hours together had been in there. Memories flashed through my mind, like a movie stuck on a loop. Precious moments before turmoil hit.

Edging closer to the door–All the little things, the simple daily occurrences I took for granted, bombarded me. The joy in Dad's voice. The sparkle in his deep brown eyes when I agreed to join him on the last hunt.

If I had known that would be our last day together, I would have done things differently. *Damn, why is this so hard?* We shared many journeys side by side, that's why. Mom died when I was eleven, and Dad had been my everything ever since. Father. Protector. Mentor. Best friend.

Three months had passed since his death, but that didn't stop people from contacting the Direwolf Bounty hunter Agency. Every call reminded me of the emptiness he left behind, and it was like a knife being twisted around in my heart.

They needed *his* help, expertise, and abilities, but all they got was drunk ass me. What did these people expect? They had certain demands I wasn't sure I could meet. I hadn't even had time to process that Dad was gone, and not coming back. I grappled with everyday life, barely functioning as I traveled through a never-ending fog of grief. Swallowing my fear, I reached out–hand shaking as I grasped the doorknob.

When I didn't move, Fenris let out a soft whine, then

pushed his snout into my back, and nudged me forward. My furry companion, who appeared as a husky to the world, had a way of sensing my emotions.

My top teeth sunk deep into my bottom lip, the taste of iron on my tongue. Exhaling the air in my lungs, I shoved the door wide open. I flipped on the light switch. The fluorescent lights flickered to life, illuminating the destruction inside.

The office lay in shambles. Piles of paperwork littered both desks. A mound of dirty dishes from the last time I was here were still in the sink, and the pungent aroma of garbage lingered in the air. The smells overwhelmed my senses, making my stomach churn. Bile tickled the back of my throat as I trudged through the mess. *Wow! This is disgusting.*

The moment I stepped past the threshold, the phone rang. *Did they sense my arrival the second I walked inside?*

"Gah, you've got to be kidding me! One step back into the office and it's like everyone knows I'm here. They can leave a damn message."

Ignoring the phone, I focused on the task ahead. I needed

to organize myself before I could take cases again. How would I do this without Dad? My chest tightened and I cleared my throat. Glancing at his empty desk, I closed my eyes. Patting my pocket, I felt for the key Dad handed to me as he took his final breaths.

Sensing my emotions, Fenris sauntered over to me, licked my hand, and plopped down on his bed near the desk. His glamor form shimmered away, revealing a massive Timberwolf with large amber eyes. The silvery gray and white hairs gave way to inky black fur while the blue of his irises glittered to a golden hue.

I grinned. It was always fun to watch him shift from a fluffy, adorable husky to his true form.

Fenris wasn't an ordinary Timberwolf. Dad suspected he was the last of the Direfolk: an ancient breed of giant wolves descended from the God Fenrir—which is how he got his name. Even if it was a cliché, I didn't care. It suited him well.

Fenris's eyes followed me with this indescribable look he often gave me. We were connected, able to sense everything each other felt. He completed my soul.

For the first six months of my life, I was quite ill. My tiny body struggled to survive. Nothing my parents tried helped.

But when Fenris showed up, just a pup himself, all my issues disappeared.

Mom and Dad found him curled up beside my crib sound asleep, and I was at peace for the first time since birth. I considered myself lucky. I almost lost Fenris too. The mysterious monster who killed my father attacked us first. We had no idea what we were walking into on that last hunt. This thing was like nothing we'd encountered before. Honestly surprised we made it through.

Over the past few months, I neglected him. *Shit, I'm a total asshole. I don't deserve his love or loyalty.* I needed to make it up to him somehow. He was the reason I was alive.

Fenris had tried to save Dad after protecting me, but he was too injured to get to him in time.

The beast's jagged claws tore into my side, but he fought it off. My eyes locked on the creature as it hovered over him. Then

Dad fired a shot, moving its focus off us and onto him. My adrenaline kicked in. I checked on Fenris before I joined my dad, but it was too late.

Pebbles and loose dirt bounced around my feet. Lionlike paws with curved nails peeked out from a single storm cloud, shrouding most of the beast's body. I wobbled back and forth. The ground quaked beneath us. The size and sheer force of the beast rushing toward my father knocked me down face first. I scrambled up to my feet. Pain seared up my left ribs and then...

I shuddered at the memory of what I saw next. It scratched at the edges of my mind. Determined to curb the vision, I shoved it back away.

Fenris tilted his head in my direction, which left me speculating if he heard pieces of my thoughts again. After Dad passed away, we lost some of our telepathic communication abilities. I hoped this was a sign that it was returning. Despite my best efforts, I was never able to establish a connection as strong as Fenris.

Apprehension took hold, and tears stung my eyes. "Do

I have what it takes? Am I strong enough to run DBA on my own?" The question scraped past my throat, raw from holding back the emotions that threatened to overflow.

"You are capable. You are your father's daughter." Fenris's deep, booming voice pierced the air with each word.

I crinkled up my nose, not as convinced as he was. "I hope you're right."

"I am certain of it," he replied.

"Let's hope that statement doesn't bite us in the ass later. First thing that needs to happen is tidying up the place." I rolled up my sleeves, ready to clean. Part of me thought cleaning would clear my head and prepare me for dealing with the mundane chore of filing old cases.

Running my fingers over the rough edges of scattered piles of paperwork, I groaned. Though I knew better, I secretly wished I could toss them all out. The notes within were invaluable, but I always enjoyed being out on the job more. Even emptying the trash and washing dishes was more appealing than sorting through those files.

My hangover from the night before pounded against my skull. I reached for the bottle of ibuprofen and took four pills, hoping to ease my throbbing headache.

The odor of stale and moldy food was inescapable, so I disposed of the garbage, then filled the sink with water and carefully scrubbed each dish. It was gross work, but oddly satisfying when I finished the task.

An hour passed. I put the dried dishes away in the cabinet and tucked the chairs in around the break table in the back. Dusting off my hands on my pant leg, I headed to the front desks. Being sober sucked ass. Sadness twisted around me like a boa constrictor with its prey. Grief had been a tricky beast for me. And I hadn't dealt with it in the best way. The past month was a total blur. Each night, I drank myself into oblivion then found solace in the nearest warm body. And lately, that body had been the demon, Abraxas. All of it numbed my pain and dissipated the memories. Only it never lasted long enough.

When I sobered up, I wallowed in self-hate and misery with a hangover for days. Then, when I couldn't handle the barrage of feelings anymore, I'd crack another drink open and head out to the club.

That is until uncle John showed up. He wasn't related to us, but he was family in every way that counted. Dad and I never subscribed to the idea that family was kin. Family was more than the stuff flowing through our veins.

Right before the next bottle grazed my lips, John snatched it away and knocked the sense back into me. *"You won't find your dad's killer if you keep this up. You'll be as good as dead when the next monster rolls into town."*

The tears I had been fighting to conceal escaped, and I could no longer contain my grief. Every night my mind plagued me with the same nightmare: the harrowing sight of my dad being slaughtered by that malevolent creature—with large, luminous red eyes staring right at me. Those eyes haunted me even when I was awake.

"You don't know my pain!" My body shook.

"Aaima, I understand your sorrow. Every hunter has a traumatic experience that sent them down this path. Trust me, I'll never forget walking in on my family being butchered by vampires. Don't let your grief overpower you, please."He wrapped an arm around my shoulders to comfort me.

I apologized because if anyone could relate to the agony of losing someone they love; it was John. He wasn't raised in this life like I was, but had been thrust into it after a rogue vamp coven killed his entire family. John had vowed the night his family died that he'd make it up to them somehow by helping others. Dad had saved him, and from then on, they hunted together.

He'd been a part of our lives ever since. There wasn't a hunt my dad took on that he missed. It didn't take long before John became like family to us.

I wanted revenge on the thing that ripped my father away from me. So, I intended to go back to the exact spot where he died, and follow whatever traces I could find, even if they led me back to death's doorstep. I had been there once. On the brink, slipping further across the veil. And I would do it again.

John thought I was being impulsive and stupid. He begged me to see things with clarity—without the booze clouding my judgment.

He said something wasn't quite right with our last mission. My dad rarely made mistakes. He was right. Which made me believe that someone set us up. But who? And why? I needed to find out.

I thumbed through the stacks of documents on my desk in search of answers. Even if I found something, this was going to take forever. No way I could pull off two jobs at the same time. I needed an assistant asap, and I knew exactly who to call—the person I trusted most.

I picked up the phone and dialed Abraxas's number, perching on the edge of my desk, and twirled the cord around my fingers as I waited for him to answer.

There was a click and a rustle of fabric, but I didn't wait for him to speak before saying, "Hey, my man! It's Aaima, I'm looking for a new assistant for the office, someone easy to work with. Their tasks would be to take calls, file a shit ton of paperwork, do some light cleaning, and maybe help with a few cases? Got anyone who fits?"

"Back to work already?" he asked in a strained voice.

I could almost see those lips of his pressed into a hard line as I gripped the phone tighter and let out a hesitated sigh.

"Someone's gotta do it." I huffed with more irritation than I wanted.

"Are you sure you're ready for this?" he asked, his tone heavy with concern. I breathed in hard and released my breath slowly before answering him.

"Don't fret, I can handle myself." Despite my growing

uncertainty, I put on a confident tone and forced a smile, knowing that he wouldn't be able to see it.

He sighed softly, his voice lowering as he spoke, "Please, be careful."

"Don't worry your pretty little demon head over me. I'll be fine." His lack of faith in me stung, and I couldn't help biting out, "So, do you have someone or not?"

"Hmm. The moment I mention the DBA, they're probably going to say no," he warned.

He was right; our reputation proceeded us and a lot of Sups outright refused to work for us. The job had certain risks, even with it being mostly office work.

I chewed on my bottom lip, considering his words. "C'mon, there must be someone. How about not mentioning the DBA?" I teased, tapping my fingers on the desk. The clicking sound grounded me in the present.

"I'm thinking, one second...." The sound of papers shifted in the background. "Ah! I got it! New kid, a banshee, a perfect fit for the job. Want me to send him over?"

My fingers stopped their rhythmic tapping. "*Him*? Like a male banshee? How is that even possible?"

"Do you have any issues with giving him a chance? Everyone else has declined, and he's desperate, so he'll probably say yes—even if I mention the DBA."

"Nope." I announced, making the *P* pop. "No issues whatsoever. If you say he's up for the task, I'll hire him. Tell him he has a job if he wants it. What's his name?"

"Don't laugh." His deep voice warned.

I hesitated, emotions warring as I wondered what that statement could mean. Why would I laugh at a name? "Um, okay?"

"He insists his name is Specter. Aaima, I had to keep myself from laughing." He laughed into the phone loud enough I pulled it briefly away before waiting until he was finished, then pressed it back to my ear. "That was the best alias he could come up with? Does he think I'm an idiot?"

I snorted, "Well, tell banshee boy to come by the office if he's around. Or I'll see him tomorrow at 9 a.m. sharp—no, scratch that, better make it 10."

"Big plans tonight? Don't party too hard," Abraxas chuckled.

"No, my party days are over," I sighed, disappointed I had to actually adult. Adulting was overrated. "I'm cleaning up my act."

"Heh, heard that before." There was a brief pause before he added, "Are we not going to have fun together anymore? I'll miss being in between those sweet legs of yours."

"You pig." I feigned disgust, but a flush of warmth flooded my pelvic region at the thought of his touch.

"A pig can wish," he murmured.

Just the sound of his voice deepening sent tingles throughout my body. I shut it down before answering. "Who knows? You might just get lucky. If you promise to do what you did last time with that talented tongue of yours," I teased.

"Mmm, it's a deal." He sounded a little too sure of himself.

"You don't need that written in blood, do you?" My pulse sped up. I hated writing shit in blood. It was too final. Not that I was being serious, but with demons... well, you never knew. It was always better to play the game carefully.

"For you, I'll let the contract slide."

"Okay, sweet cheeks, thanks for the help. See ya on the flip side."

"Or the horizontal side if my wish comes true," he said, a sly tone in his voice.

"Such a charmer... you just might," I said, but the words were strained as I held back. Damn him. He knew how to get me right where he wanted me.

His voice turned even more sultry, caressing me through the phone, transforming that heat into an inferno. "Looking forward to it."

"I bet you are. Can we talk more about us later?" My curiosity piqued; I wondered what he'd say next. Brax paused, and the silence stretched on for what felt like an eternity.

"*Us*, you say?" he made a low humming sound, deep in his throat. "Yes, I'd like that. Bye, babe."

"Bye." I breathed into the phone, realizing that I was playing a dangerous game and god, it felt so good.

My hips tingled at the image of Brax against my core, as his lips kissed my neck. I longed for the fire that raged in me when we connected.I couldn't ignore the invisible bond that always brought us back together, no matter what obstacles we faced. It made me wonder if I could—or should—give him my heart.

My thoughts returned to my dad. He loved me unconditionally, but I doubt he'd approve of his daughter dating a demon. *Especially* if that demon was Abraxas. It's not that Dad didn't trust him, but he warned me Brax would always choose neutrality over taking sides. Even mine, if we ever had something serious develop between us.

I couldn't blame Abraxas. I understood the supernatural world had to be kept under wraps. Truth was, he worked both sides just enough to keep a balance. He understood the equilibrium that kept our community safe. Guess dad didn't want my heart crushed if Brax chose the comfort of his game over me.

Yet here I was, ready to tell him how I truly felt. Fenris shot an angry look my way, then proceeded to ignore me for almost half an hour. He hated demons, something he was always quick to remind me of.

I rolled my eyes before organizing the files on the break table.

As much as Fenris detested them, he realized Abraxas wasn't all bad. *Easy on the eyes, too.*

It's not like I wanted to settle down and have a family with Brax. At least if I did, they would have the advantage of being half-human-half-demon.

I wouldn't want my kids in this business though. This line of work cost my family their lives. I hadn't heard from my other family members in years, so I assumed the worst at this point. Sometimes I wondered why we hunters continued to do what we did. Death followed us everywhere. Most never made it past the age of forty. Some of us were luckier than others, but I considered that more of a fluke than anything.

Some hunters had something supernatural lurking in their

DNA, which gave them a small advantage when dealing with the things that go bump in the night. My family had been the supernatural police for centuries because we had more Sup in our human veins than most. Everyone in the community heard of us.

At one point, I had wanted out, but Dad begged me to reconsider and practically dragged me along on the last hunt.

It was another reason his death continued to eat at me. Part of me held myself responsible for what happened.

I wish I had been more aware of what was going on. Dad taught me well, but I spent two years wasting my time trying to be 'normal.'

Except, once you're in this life, it's hard to find your way out.

Chapter Two

First Day Back: Part Two

Aaima

Maybe Dad would still be alive if I stayed hunting with him instead of going to college.

The monster slipped in and out of our reality, cloaked in a dense storm cloud. I was rusty, and that thing was unlike anything I had faced before.

With powers like that, we never stood a chance. We had our usual weapons, pistols, shotguns, and a few swords. They barely touched this thing. Not even the spells we knew had affected it.

I pushed back from the desk and scrubbed my face. After a couple of hours of attempting to dig through the scrambled paperwork for more information on the monster, I came up with exactly zilch. I couldn't think past the fog of grief long enough to focus. Heartache consumed me, blinding me in ways I hadn't expected. There was only one place I still needed to look. My gaze slid to the lock on Dad's private filing cabinet.

I'd been avoiding it all day. Even with him gone, my nerves got to me. Everything in there was always off limits, *not until the right time,* Dad had said.

Pursing my lips, I wished he was here for this. I jiggled the small key until the first drawer of the cabinet creaked open. Everything was chock-full, folder after folder, untidy, like he had been in a rush the last time he closed it up.

"Wow. I can't tell what's what. This wasn't like him at all."

"No, it wasn't. He was meticulous with records. Are we sure no one else has been here?" Fenris asked as he got up and padded over to me.

"I don't think so because he locked it. Also, you're the one with the super sense of smell, you tell me." I frowned, not liking the feeling that tied my stomach into knots.

"Between the lingering stench and previous clients, I'm unable to identify anything I haven't already smelled," he said.

I slammed my fist into the cabinet drawer. "We don't have time to waste sorting through this. Finding the person who killed Dad is our top priority." My jaw ached from clenching my teeth so hard.

Reluctantly, I reached for the stack of files then meandered over to the break table and plopped the thick pile down.

Slouching over the mound of papers, I muttered, "Impossible."

The task ahead would test me far more than I felt ready for. These files... all this paperwork... they were merely the beginning.

A pain in the ass too.

Fenris followed me and continued, "When does this assistant arrive? Are you sure a banshee will be helpful?" he flicked his head to the side.

"I think so. At least, if something happens. It's not like he can actually die." I shrugged, not looking up from the file I was leafing through.

Fenris licked his lips. His teeth glittered in the sunlight shining through the window, and his bright eyes fixated on me. "That's true. In this business, we don't always know what we are up against. No one's ever heard of a male banshee before. For all we know, he could bring nothing but trouble."

"Then we'll deal with it when it happens. Listen, he'll be able to disappear on sight if someone comes looking for us. I also heard some banshees are twice as fast as others. Let's hope that's true." I paced the room, squeezing, then releasing my fists. My six sense prickled my flesh. "My gut tells me the last fight was only the beginning. Whatever we discover next will change a lot of things for us. But no matter what, we'll find out who's behind this."

“Can’t wait. They’ll learn what true regret is when I sink my teeth into their neck and rip out their spine,” Fenris growled.

I grabbed more disheveled folders out of the drawers, heading back to the break table that would serve as my work area for the week.

“I think all of your dad’s private files need to be opened, and that includes the cabinet downstairs.” Fenris pointed his slick black nose to the back room.

“Oh shit! I forgot about those. This means I need to check Dad’s desk for all of his keys.” I walked over and sat down in the chair, wondering which drawer held the rest of his secrets from me.

Before searching, I took a moment to bask in the room’s stillness. This had been Dad’s view for years and it was strange to me he’d never sit here again. Once opened, I couldn’t find anything that caught my attention. Nothing but labeled files, the money lockbox, pens, and blank notebooks. Most people kept the keys in the top ones. But Dad was anything but typical.

The bottom drawer was the only one I hadn't tried because it was locked. My pulse sped up and I pulled the blood-stained key from my pocket.

This has to be it. I hesitated for a long moment before inserting it into the keyhole, but I didn't turn it. Something didn't feel right.

As much as I didn't want to do this without him, I knew I had to. There was no other choice, and I hated it.

I froze, the metal of the key biting into my palm as I forced myself to turn it slowly in the lock. The drawer clicked open, breaking the silence. It was now or never.

What lied inside? Would I be any closer to the answers I sought? Or would I be drowning in more clues? *More lies?*

Finish this Aaima, I love you. His last words echoed in my mind, making me feel even more uneasy. The truth was about to unravel before me, and I knew it.

All I had to do now was open the drawer.

CHAPTER THREE

BANSHEE BOY

Aaima

Peeking inside the drawer, I frowned down at the collection of random items–haphazardly laying inside with a velvet cloth underneath. I arranged them on the desk. Keys, talismans, and leather-bound books. These had to be Dad's recent journals. I pushed the artifacts to the side and set the books in the center, then gripped the edge of the desk. I was eager to explore Dad's final writings and the records he hadn't let me touch before.

"Your dad's journals?" Fenris asked.

"Yes, let's dive in." I replied, then began flipping through several pages of the journal on top. "Want me to order some food?"

"Please, or glamor me, so I can hunt in the woods." Fenris propped his large paws on the desk and licked the side of my face.

I came to a halt and fixed my eyes on him. "While I do enjoy seeing you as a cute little husky—it's a no. Not until I know we're safe here. I'll take a cue from Dad and err on the side of caution. You okay with that? Deal?"

"Deal," he said, staring me down before I reached for the phone.

Fenris wanted raw meat but could tolerate some cooked meals here and there. Surprised that he didn't argue, I scanned our menus quick. Ultimately, I decided I didn't feel like grabbing takeout. So I ordered my favorite delivery place, Magu's Wok.

"Hey, Jai. Usual order of chicken cooked up plain, lots of

veggies, hold the sauce. Yep, that's for Fenris. Yeah, I'm back to work. Thirty minutes? Cool, thanks."

I wanted to see how far I could get before the food arrived. The page I opened it to was this year's first entry. Dad had written something about me after he detailed the table of contents in the front. I cringed.

He questioned if I was ready for the truth, saying he needed to prepare me for what was coming, but I kept resisting.

...if only she would stop resisting. As it is, I don't know if she'll be able to handle S.S.

I paused at the set of initials. *S.S.* was obviously code for something. I quickly flipped through several pages, but there was nothing mentioning who, or what, the letters stood for.

Coupled with the cryptic message written at the beginning, I had to wonder who he was talking about. I paused for a second. Answers were probably tucked away throughout; waiting for the person who took time to search for them.

The entry ended with words that weighed heavily on my mind.

Something is coming... I feel it in my gut. If Aaima isn't ready in time, it will be the end of our line, and that is exactly what they want.

The next several entries after that were our typical hunting cases. Dad was always meticulous with details. There were twelve pages of notes for the case dealing with poltergeists other hunters struggled to get rid of before Dad had even set foot out of the office.

Unfortunately, I didn't find a single hint that would bring me closer to an answer to my questions.

I stood and straightened my jeans. There was a ton of research to do. *I'm going to have to spend the night here.* I went downstairs for a minute to prep the full-size bed for the night. Shaking out the bedding before I came back up.

I contemplated dropping my monthly lease. Move in permanently. It would be easier and save on cash too. We kept money from the front office separate from our supernatural bounties and hunting trips. David, our manager from that section of our company–had a good handle on our business front. And I wanted to keep it that way. I didn't want to pull funds from there. I wasn't low on cash, but until I got into the groove with clients, I'd have to pinch those pennies.

Sitting back down, I continued my search for clues.

I heard the hum of an engine pull up. Food was here. The door to the office swung open and in stepped Jai with another person.

There were four bags of food in her hands. She sat them down on my desk and looked at me, a bright smile on her face. "Good to have ya back. I have extra pot stickers and a special treat for someone." She beamed.

"Thanks, I missed you! How've you been? How's your mom doing?" I scooped the bags up and headed to the back-room. Jai followed.

"She's good, wouldn't stop talking about you when she saw your order come in."

I gave her a quick glance before setting the food on the other end of the table. *Can't muck those files up with soy sauce.* Jai was a sup. It surprised me she didn't even notice the tall, lanky fellow who came in behind her.

This had to be the banshee Brax sent over. He was hiding out in his ethereal form. Specters could conceal themselves from almost anyone except me.

As Jai continued to talk, he moved off to the right and stood still. I tilted my head to one side and studied him. He had no clue I locked my sights on him. Jai kept jabbering. I smirked. *This is fun.*

"She tucked a new dessert in there for you too. Best cake you'll ever have. Hey, what are you looking at? You're distracted this evening." She glanced over her shoulder and back at me.

"No, not distracted. Thought I saw someone else come in with you." the banshee's eyes widened, and he tried his best to blend into the wall. I turned my attention back to her.

"Oh! Nope, just me tonight." She rocked back and forth on her toes.

"Tell your mom she's the best! I'll stop by to see her soon. Can't wait to try the new cake she's made." I took some chopsticks out of their wrapper, cracked them in half, and rubbed them together. I was ready to dig in.

"Sure thing." she glanced down at her watch. "Well, I better get going. More deliveries."

"Darn. Was hoping you had a few minutes to burn. Next time call me before your break? Get my order in so we can hang out for a bit?"

"Hells yes! If you need anything else, let me know." She gave me a quick hug, and I squeezed her back.

"Of course I will, and thank you." my eyes followed her out the door.

When she was gone, I turned to face the banshee. "Are you going to gloom about all afternoon or properly introduce yourself?" my eyebrow tweaked up as I made eye contact with him.

His mouth gaped, and he stuttered, "Y-You can see me, but you're human? The Xian didn't even notice my presence."

I giggled. "Well, banshee boy, not sure what to tell you other than it's one of my gifts. If you're of the ghost variety, there's no hiding from me. Also color me impressed. Few people can spot a Xian."

He tried to apologize for what he said, like pointing out I was human. Poor thing fumbled over his words once more before taking corporeal form–his skin changed from a translucent blue to a pale ivory. Now that was something I hadn't seen before. I motioned for him to sit, and he slumped onto the couch nearest to him.

"Sorry, I'm just nervous. No one seems to want me around, like I'm a bad omen or something." He stared down at his hands, twiddling his thumbs together before looking back up at me.

"You're a male banshee. How'd you think most in our community would react?" I crossed my arms, focusing on his every move. I could tell something bad happened to him and wondered what exactly.

"To be honest, I'm not sure." He fumbled with the button on his blazer before looking at me directly.

"One thing you need to learn right now, Specter. Speaking

of that... come on, tell me your real name."

"It's Stefen," he whispered.

"So, out of all the aliases to choose from, you went with the cheesiest?" I chortled. Slapping my hand on my leg as a wide smile crossed my face.

He fiddled with his glasses, his fingers trembling and voice breaking. "I was nervous. My mother warned me to never tell a demon my real name."

"She's right and wrong. But really, Is Specter the best you could come up with? Brax knows that's not your real name." pausing I smirked and winked in his direction before continuing. Letting the sharpness fade from my voice, I spoke more gently and asked, "Oh, do you mind if I call you Stef for short?"

"Not at all. And you're probably right, but he didn't press the issue."

"He's cool like that. By the way, are you hungry? There's plenty here for everyone." I directed his attention to the food on the break table and propped open the pot stickers, taking one and plopping it into my mouth. Hunger gnawed at my stomach, and it growled in protest.

Stef laughed softly in response to my tummy's protests. "Oh, gods yes! But I don't want to intrude on your dinner."

"Dude, you're good. Dig in, my friend."

Stefen looked mighty confused. "What about an interview?"

"You slipped in undetected, you're undead, and no one else ever sticks around long enough to finish the job, anyway. So, you're hired." I shrugged.

"Um, are you sure?" He cocked an eyebrow.

"You good at answering phones? Sorting files? Cleaning up a bit?" I asked.

"Yes." Stef's lips pursed as he leaned his head to the side.

The side of my mouth ticked up in amusement. "You able to hide at a moment's notice?"

"Uh...y-yes." He cleared his throat several times while fumbling back and forth on his feet. His nerves getting the best of him.

I sighed, knowing that Brax hadn't given Stef the proper details. Softening my tone I asked, "Abraxas told you the bare minimum about this job, huh?"

"He told me you needed an assistant, mostly office work, and maybe some help with cases. I didn't ask him to elaborate." He gulped as his shoulders shrunk down and he continued to squirm in his seat.

I rubbed my temples. "Did he tell you who I was?" I wasn't sure why I asked, because I was positive that I already knew the answer.

"No. Said he had a job for me, and I didn't question it."

And my gut was right. Brax hadn't said a damn word about DBA to this unsuspecting noob. I shook my head. Damned demon knew I was joking. I glanced up, hoping Stef would stay once I told him.

"Did you even read the sign outside? It's a bit worn out and hard to read if you're not looking, even so," I asked first, before dropping our business name.

He looked down at his feet and shook his head no. I'm

sorry, I desperately need this job.

Before I could say another word, Fenris stretched and stood up. His head was a few inches above my elbow. His height scared many people off since I was 5'10. Stefen's movements were clumsy as he backed away, his face an even paler shade than before.

His voice shrilled. "Holy Hades! A Direwolf! This is... this is... Direwolf Bounty hunter Agency."

"Sure is."

"Your dad was Assad." He bowed his head low before he glanced back up at me. "I'm so sorry for your loss."

Man, who didn't know about Dad in this town? I loved that Dad's kindness and willingness to help left an impression on everyone. Including individuals I was unfamiliar with.

"Thanks, I'm sorry Brax didn't tell you. I thought he knew I was joking about leaving that part out when trying to find me an assistant. Are you going to leave now? I wouldn't blame you."

"No, I'll stay," he said.

"Cool, my name is Aaima. This is Fenris."

Stefen cowered when Fenris got close enough to touch him. Couldn't say I blamed him. Everything about Fenris was unsettling. Personally, I loved it.

"Don't worry, Fenris is a big softie." I laughed.

"He's huge!" he said, with his arms out wide.

"Meh, soon you won't even notice. So, you're for sure taking the job?" I eyed Stef closely while he paused. No doubt he was thinking about his answer before he spoke.

"Yes."

"Even if it's dangerous?" I tweaked up an eyebrow, studying his every move.

"I thought it was office work?" he grimaced, wringing his hands together.

"Yes, and no. There might be times I need you on a case with me. I promise you won't be unprepared." I paused, scanning his movements. He wiggled uncomfortably in his seat and pushed the rim of his glasses back up his nose before taking in a deep breath. I finally broke the awkward silence that settled between us. "Don't worry, I'll get you ready beforehand."

"I am sure I can handle it." He straightened his spine and sat upright.

I liked the show of confidence and smiled. "Good, now let's eat first, then get to work."

Stefen nodded while I handed him a plate and utensils. He added small portions of fried rice, orange chicken, and took a slice of cake. I came in right after him, heaping the food into tiny mountains on mine before I continued to give him the rundown.

"Oh, and I'll split my earnings with you, that sound good?"

"Yeah, I think. I've never had a job before."

"You'll get the hang of it in no time and the money is good." "I'm thinking we start with this filing cabinet here." I directed his attention to the one I had been cleaning out earlier. "Also, are you staying somewhere close by? How'd you get here? You okay to work for about an hour, then head out after that? Longer if you feel up to it?" I unloaded all the questions on him and regretted it. Poor kid clamped up and stood there stiff as a corpse. Which made me bite my lip, so I didn't laugh out loud–him being undead and all.

Stef winced, his voice shaking. "Uh... I-I'll be okay. I can find a spot."

I instantly changed my tone. He was not okay, and I wanted to know what happened to him. "If you don't have a proper place to stay, there's a small room with a twin bed in the back. It's yours if you'd like it. Now I know why Brax sent you my way."

He let out a long sigh. "Thank you. I really don't have anywhere to go right now, but are you sure you want me to stay here? We just met."

I cackled, "You don't appear the type to burn your bridges, so yes. Plus, screw me over and I'll hunt you down and kick your ass. We've always helped dislocated Sups when needed. Let's eat and continue to discuss."

Stef watched me scarf down my food. He seemed shocked, maybe impressed. "What? Never seen a girl eat before?"

"Well, not like that," he chuckled.

Fenris laughed, then said he had seen nothing yet. I thought poor Stefen was going to soil his banshee pants.

"He can talk? What!? Why? How?"

"Yep." I watched Fenris study Stefen's face.

"How is he able to talk?" he muttered while Fenris continued to watch his reactions.

"My dad told me he's the spawn of a God, so he's able to speak. He appears to be a wolf, but he's always been more."

"Whoa. Cool. I should have paid more attention to that section on godlike beings in homeschool."

"You'll get first-hand experience now, better than a textbook. Can you tell me more about yourself? Where are you from?" I asked.

"Here. My mom and I lived on an estate outside of the city. I wasn't allowed to leave, though. Then one day she was... uh... she disappeared. I have been alone ever since."

"Damn. Sorry, what do you mean disappeared? Like abandoned you or did someone take her? Is your place not safe?"

“It’s hard to talk about right now,” he replied.

I noted his body language. Stef clasped his hands behind him while his head tilted down. The grave expression on his face when he looked up told me something terrible had happened. He was hesitant to trust. I understood where he was coming from and wouldn’t press the issue. “Take your time. A portion of my cases are tracking down missing Sups. It happens more often than our community thinks. Seriously, once you’re ready, let’s see if we can find your mom.”

“No, I wasn’t aware. I thought the DBHA was mostly hunting down rogue Supernaturals, so the humans don’t catch wind of us.”

“Just DBA.” I suggested, “We work with bail bonds and private investigations on the human side. Mostly, we keep our ears open for those unusual cases or we get hired to take down or bring in rogue members of the community.”

“Oh? Interesting? Can I ask why the H is dropped?”

“Sure can. My dad kept running into people stumbling over the ‘H’ in DBHA. So he started calling it the DBA and it stuck."

"Oh. That makes sense. Yeah, okay, that sounds good. Yes, tell me what you need me to do."

"Office needs to be clean and presentable, but that is a task for tomorrow. I got the nasty stuff, like the dishes and trash. Right now, it's paperwork. See all those stacks on that table over there? You need to go through them and separate by date."

"Yes ma'am, err, I mean boss. Sorry. I'll get this going," he sputtered.

"Brax was right. You're a decent kid."

"I'm eighteen." Stef scowled.

"KID." I goaded him on a little. All in good fun, of course.

"Well, how much older are you then?" he asked.

I glared at him and pointed toward my old desk. He got the drift and shuffled along before he sat down. He put his plate down in from him and glanced up as he waited for my answer.

"I'm twenty-two and a half, but I've been working bounties and cases since I was thirteen."

"I see."

"And you've been housebound until now?"

He looked a little embarrassed and tucked his chin to his chest.

"Listen, what I mean is inexperienced. I won't call you a kid again, I promise. But you have a lot to learn, especially if you are on your own being a male banshee. I can't say for certain who might come after you, but trust me, there are things out there that would love to get their hands on you and figure out what makes you tick."

He sighed. "You're right. My mom said the same thing."

"When you get a chance, you need to thank Brax too. I can guarantee he's had his bodyguard, Braun, watching over you until you arrived. He knows how the darker side works. I get why your mom kept you a secret–to protect you. She probably thought it was best to keep you hidden. Personally, I think it's important for you to learn how to defend yourself."

He cleared his throat. "I agree with you. Can you help with that?"

"Sure thing. We'll start small and work our way up. Oh, and Stef, how fast can you read?" I had to ask. I wanted to see how quickly we could get through Dad's files.

"Well, pretty fast. I'm a banshee, after all. It's one of our talents."

"Good. Scan all those documents, take thorough notes on anything that seems out of place or needs to be brought to my attention, okay?"

"Anything in particular?"

"Yes. I am trying to find out who killed my father and why. If anything feels off or out-of-place write it down."

He nodded, not saying another word, and started sorting through papers right away.

Stef didn't eat as much as I did. He was moving swiftly in between bites of food. I hadn't been this up-close to a banshee working before. I watched him flip through pages like a speed demon. His hands were a blur. *Remarkable.* I heard banshees were quick and had seen one work for Brax at his club briefly–at a distance. But Stef was moving much faster than she was.

I emptied the two boxes of chicken and vegetables into a large bowl near Fenris's water source. Then, I returned to reading Dad's last journal entry:

I struggled to convince Aaima to join me on the last bounty. She's stubborn as hell. I am not sure when she started hating the job so much. She's been in this community for too long. She needs to understand this is the way it has always been for hunters. We keep the supernatural world in check.

She doesn't understand how important she is. It's my fault. I need to tell her about her lineage. There's so much I haven't shared, but I will soon. I can't write what it is in this book, but I'm going to tell John before we head out on this hunt.

Something is still bothering me.

I've been thinking about that vamp Matthias and why Victor wants him dead. If my information is correct, they're related. There's more happening behind the scenes there. Maybe Abraxas knows something. I can't find this vampire anywhere to question him despite helping him earlier.

I wonder if Victor is plotting something big. Occasionally, you get a vamp who thinks they can control the human world. No idea if that's his end goal for his coven, Sanguine Sanctum. But I need to find out. From my experience, many Sups may consider humans weak, but they outnumber the supernatural community.

They'd do well to heed what I've said for years! Eventually, they'd retaliate. Sure, Supernaturals may fascinate them, but humans have a way of destroying things like nothing I've ever seen before. Someday I hope Aaima will see why it's so important before it is too late.

Fear sits in my belly as I write this. Something is amiss, and soon it will rear its ugly head in our direction. I am the longest living hunter out there. I'm 200 years old. And I haven't told Aaima yet. I've kept it a secret all these years. Need to tell her everything soon.

I had to stop reading. *Dad was how old? What the hells? What did he mean by our kind? Why did he keep this from me? Why would he hide it in the first place?* There had been whispers over the years that we were more than human hunters with a smidge of Sup in our blood, but I always brushed it off as gossip. We were good at our jobs, that's all.

I had more questions than answers now, so I did the only thing I could and kept reading. Several entries randomly mentioned Sanguine Sanctum or had those initials *S.S.* Even when it didn't relate to the case. Or maybe it did, and I wasn't seeing the connection right away. The next entry took a different direction. Dad was talking about me again. I swallowed hard before reading on.

As I read more about my behavior of ignoring him and making him sad, I felt a twinge of guilt. He knew it was my age. A time everyone rebelled against their parents. He knew I had to find my way. He was certain I'd come through for him later. But I failed him. He died holding onto secrets I couldn't begin to understand, and the monster that killed him was still out there.

Whoever, whatever, wanted to make sure he was out of the picture. I bet they thought we'd all be dead after our last hunt together.

I'd show them. Part of me knew it was wrong, but vengeance coiled around me and took hold. I might have stepped away to figure myself out. One thing I wasn't was a coward. I'd confront the enemy head on. My father taught me to confront fear as if it were a tangible being, and that's exactly what I did. *"Fear helps our awareness,"* he always said. Fear kept a person cautious. In this line of work, jumping in head-first could get you or your partner killed.

Hunters needed to watch, wait, and listen. They needed to gather every scrap of detail in silence. Take in their surroundings, the scents, and soul marks. The smallest thing might help a hunt succeed.

Many of our bounties were for Supernaturals out of control. A lot of them looked human and acted like it too, but then there were the others. They were the true monsters, the ones you read about in ancient myths and folktales. Except they were all very real and deadly.

I finished reading the last passage he wrote.

She has a natural talent within her. Her sixth sense is twice as powerful as mine. She gets it from her mother I am glad she had magic that passed down to Aaima. I miss Isabelle. My heart will never fully recover from losing her. This is why it's so hard to have my daughter distance herself from me. She's the only good thing I've added to this world. Reflecting on her childhood and teen years, I realize I went about things the wrong way. I wanted to protect her from the same fate as her mother and cousins. I wanted her to be near invincible so she would live a longer life than I. It was foolish to think that she wouldn't rebel. What young adult doesn't? For many years, I was there too. I had hundreds of years to live yet. Her mother tamed my wild ass. I am frustrated that she's more like me than I care to admit.

Dad thought I was like him? I teared up. Our fights didn't diminish the fact that I looked up to him. I wanted to match his strength and determination. Again, I knew he didn't like some things I did, but he was never ugly about it. He always told me, *"Do good and nothing else."* I missed the old man. Dad was my rock, even when I was being foolish and stubborn. He hadn't turned his back on me once.

With a determined mindset, I shook my thoughts off and focused. I wrote *Sanguine Sanctum* down.

Dad suspected they were monitoring him after he turned down their last bounty offer to kill Matthias for them, but my dad wouldn't do it. The vamp was innocent.

"You're insane, Victor. I won't go after a vampire who hasn't broken sanctions. End of story. Don't call me again," Dad said. I remembered him slamming the phone done and pacing the office in silence. This had to be the clue I was looking for. I needed to figure out why this coven had a hand in half of our cases and fast.

The worst part was I had been blind to it. How did I miss this pattern? No more hard partying for me. I needed complete clarity. Vamps were tricky. I needed to devise ways to spy on them. I could ask Stef to help me with recon. *Gah! Is that a good idea?*

He'd be able to sneak in undetected. But we just met and he was fresh out of momma's womb or might as well have been.

Chapter Four

The Mutual Connection

Aaima

Two days had passed, and we were still scouring documents for clues. My eyes were heavy and strained as I sifted through piles sprawled out on the table in front of me. Papers rustled, pens clicked, and keyboards clacked in a constant rhythm that seemed to stretch time.

Stefen came bounding up from downstairs with his arms full of folders. I couldn't believe what I saw. He had organized everything we had been working on over the past two days.

A small smile crept across his lips as he laid the thick binders down next to the others.

"Wow! Stef, did you stay up last night doing this?" I rushed over and examined them. His hard work made mine feel meaningless in comparison. But I was grateful for his skills.

"Yeah, I couldn't sleep, so I decided I'd make myself useful to keep you from firing me in the morning."

"Oh, hell no! You're a keeper, this is amazing! Thank you." I hugged him out of instinct. He froze for a second, but returned the gesture and squeezed me tight.

"You're welcome. Oh, I took notes like you asked. They're right here on this notepad." He gestured to it on the table.

I grazed over the neatly stacked files and his eloquent handwriting on each. He had labeled everything better than dad had and that was saying something. "You've outdone yourself. I'm giving you a bonus! Dinner for the rest of the month is on me."

He grinned from ear to ear. "Awesome."

I knew something bad happened to him the moment he

walked in. It was nice to see him smile. Stef still hadn't told me what happened to his mom, but he was close to opening up. Over the past few days, he had gradually opened up to me about his life. I hoped our conversations had shown him he could trust me.

I don't know if it was some sort of coincidence or mad luck. But his mom had taught him about the Supernatural world existing alongside the human populace–in great detail. He knew a lot about the creatures I hunted, possibly more. He came from an ancient line of banshees too; his mother being one of the first. I bet he'd be able to break down cases faster than I could alone.

He was a perfect fit for the job. I also squealed when he told me he loved cheesy B-rated horror films. Same as me. I swore right then he had to be the best friend I had always been looking for.

"Well, let's not waste a moment. I have some of my notes, and you have yours. Let's jump right in," I said.

We sat down at the break table, and he handed me a piece

of paper with the coven's name written at the top of it, with dates and the case name below it.

"How many times did you see Sanguine Sanctum brought up?" I asked him.

"Your father mentioned them in multiple cases, but nothing more than the abbreviation and a question mark down at the bottom for most instances. Does the coven have something to do with all those cases?"

"Possibly? I need to find something more solid than a few mentions. Where does my dad acknowledge them first?"

"The two rogue vampires with Bloodlust. They were out of control. Your dad had you take care of them instead." He slid his notebook over to me. I scanned the first sentence and looked up at him.

"Yes, I remember that case. It was January third. They thought they had me, but I beheaded them both. It was easy enough to take them down. Hmm." I paused. The whole case was odd to begin with. "Things took a weird turn. The coven wanted them brought in alive. But you can't stop a Bloodlust vampire. Death is the only choice." It was an interesting yet asinine demand on their end. And it still didn't make sense to me. "Vamps with Bloodlust will stop at nothing to satisfy their cravings. It doesn't even matter the source. They'll kill other vamps to stop their hunger. That's the problem, there's no saving them, and nothing sates their thirst. I did what I had to do."

"If they can kill other vampires, how does a hunter take them down?" Stef asked as he leaned forward, his attention solely on my words.

"Some hunters aren't the sharing type, especially the ones that have Sup in their DNA, but I'll level with you. I'm not fully a witch, but I can turn a bit of magic when I need to. My family line also has reflexes as fast, if not faster, than a vamp when adrenaline hits."

"Wow, I didn't know this."

"It's not something I openly share, for obvious reasons. I'm not the best with magic. My mom was better, but I know how to fight and fight well. The extra ump from whatever was triggered in our blood is a plus. Now, back to the cases. Things could get tricky. I want you to understand the risks, and if you choose to go, I won't hold it against you."

"No, I'm here to stay. I am done being cooped up. This is so much better than my everyday life. I hated being alone. Well, not alone, but I wanted friends. Always have."

"Yeah, I get that and hey thanks, glad you're staying put. Also, I want to train you. You have your spectral form, but if something gets the jump on you, it can weaken you in your corporeal state. We don't need that, right?"

"Right. Train me how?"

"Fighting, dodging attacks, weapons. Things like that."

"Oh, I don't think I'll be any good with that stuff. My mom only taught me how to evade danger."

"It's called learning and practice. You will surprise yourself. You underestimate your capabilities." I sounded like my dad right then, and it weirded me out. *This happens when you're sober. You sound like the old man.*

The thought tugged at my heartstrings and choked the rest

of the words right out of me. I studied Stef while he nervously went back to reading the stack of papers in front of him.

His mom was too cautious with him. I somewhat understood her stance. She had to contend with the dark underbelly of the Supernatural world while she hid from the other half–humans, or Unsups as we called them. Some hunters focused on intense cleanups for certain situations. They left no evidence behind, but the stories were there. Enough to make people question the existence of the paranormal.

Even my dad had a front for our business. He hired freelance Unsups to work bail bonds. It proved lucrative and a good addition to our private investigations. Most of the Unsups preferred bounty hunting humans to our cases any day. But they were aware of the otherworldly things around and helped on our end if we needed them to.

"I'll do my best," Stef declared.

"You will. On a side note, I failed to mention we have another office with the bail bonds. If David calls, just pass the call to me, or take a message."

"Will do." He shuffled through more files and pulled out a few, separating them from the rest. I watched him, curious what these files were. They must have had clues. I'd check later.

"So, you up for a field trip?" I asked, breaking the silence. "I want to see if we can spy on this vamp coven, but they'll smell me outright. They won't sense or see you coming."

"Are you sure about this?" his voice shook.

"This is uncharted territory. I get it. From the small bit you told me, your mom kept you tucked away in that mansion for most of your life."

"Yes, we hardly left. She said *they'd* come for me if they knew I was alive."

"Hmm, we'll have to talk about that last bit in a minute. So, here's the deal. You're technically an adult now. Your mom isn't here—you get to decide what happens next, and you have an advantage I don't. I wouldn't ask if I didn't think you were capable." He needed some courage, and quick. It was the only plan that had an advantage over the coven. Vampires were predators, and their prey was the living. They needed something physical to track, and I couldn't hide my scent.

Stefen hesitated before he opened his mouth. "Are you sure they won't sense me?"

"Trust me, vamps can't sense banshees. They're all about the blood and physical scent of a body. Gross if you ask me, but gives us the upper hand we need to succeed. If you stay in your spectral form, you'll go undetected. Gather intel and nothing more."

"This is a first for me. Are you sure you trust me to do this? This is so sudden. I've only worked here for a few days now."

"I know you can do this. Follow what I say and you'll be fine. I know we've barely met, but I feel like we are kindred spirits. No parents, no proper place in the world. I might oversee the DBA now, but this was my dad's place, his creation, not mine. It's time I make my own way and you need to do the same." I patted him on the back.

Stef lifted his chin and clamped his arms to his side. "Okay, I'm ready when you are. I was sick of hiding and now I get to make my own decisions, too." But then he fiddled with his collared shirt, his head bobbing left and right. "This is exciting, but terrifying. Oh, man! If only my mom were here, she'd freak."

"Yeah, it's interesting when you have your independence and no parent looming over your shoulder." I steadied my eye contact with him and moved closer. "Hey, before we move on to the next steps, can you disclose the details of what happened to your mom?" I paused, "It's been two days. Talk to me. I want to help."

Stef's shoulders dropped; his lips curved downward. "Why is this so hard to talk about?" he breathed out.

"It's your mom. Why would it be easy? When we figure out what happened to both our parents, I think we'll be better off."

"Agreed, you're right. Give me a second."

"Take your time." I offered. I observed him. He wasn't nervous about telling me what happened, but the pain in his eyes burned into my soul.

“There was this enormous creature outside our mansion, tearing up the gardens. My mom was out there first, but it knocked her down. I couldn’t let her fight it alone, so I rushed out, and we faced it together. The creature took a swipe at me and I wasn’t incorporeal anymore. It dragged her away, and then they vanished before I could do anything further.”

“What sort of creature?”

“That’s the thing. I remember seeing only its legs and paws clearly. It had these jagged long claws dripping poison I think? It was fast and shrouded in a storm. The clouds swirled around it like smoky tendrils. I think it has a head resembling that of a lion. I only saw half of it.” Stefen’s eyes reddened as he folded his arms, pulling them in toward his chest.

That night was etched in his mind with perfect clarity, much like how the night my dad died was seared into mine. Watching your parent get ripped away from you forever leaves a mark. Stefen had the same mark I did and his description of the creature had my hair standing on end. “Holy shit! This changes everything!” I blurted out.

"What? Do you know something about this creature?"

"Stef new mission. We need to find your mom and the thing that took her. All while continuing to gather evidence leading to my dad's killer."

"Wait, what are you talking about?"

"Things just got a lot clearer for me. That creature is the monster who attacked us and killed my dad, I'm sure of it."

His eyes widened, and he gulped loudly. "Are you serious?"

"Dead serious. The creature you described is the same one that attacked us. It moved in and out of a massive storm cloud, but never showed its complete form. Most of what I saw were its massive legs and jagged claws. It attacked me first. Fenris got the thing off me. Then I watched as it opened up my dad's torso and that's the last thing I remember before my vision blurred and I passed out." I lifted my shirt to reveal the scarred over slash marks on my ribs. "It still hurts. Whatever that beast is—it's toxic. The claws released some type of poison. I'm lucky to be alive and it hurt Fenris, which should be next to impossible."

"Damn, that's insane. Hold on, I have something to show you. Give me a second." He walked into his small room and rushed out with a sketchbook in hand, opening it square in the middle. On a page inside was the creature I saw the night Dad died.

"Wow, you're quite the artist... is that what you saw at your mansion?"

"Yes."

"It's definitely the same creature that attacked us. Can I inspect?" I reached out to grab the sketchbook from him, staring down at the image. It was the beast, but he had seen more of its face than I had. The eyes made me shudder before I talked. "Hmm, there has to be a connection here somewhere. When your mom told you about the Direwolf Bounty hunter Agency and my dad, what exactly did she say?"

Stefen shifted his feet around and looked me in the eye. "Before she even sent me to see Abraxas, she told me that if anything should happen to her, I should go to the DBA first. She said that Assad was a good man, and I could trust him.

When the creature dragged her off, she yelled out to me to find the demon Abraxas at Club Inferno, then vanished."

"Interesting. So, you went to Brax right after this happened?"

"Well, no, I asked about the DBA first, but some ghoul told me your dad died. I figured my mom must have known and sent me to Abraxas instead."

"Give me a moment to think about all of this," I said. I now had more information than I had before. This creature kidnapped a banshee and killed one of the best hunters out there. Dad also knew Stef's mom. He probably knew about Stefen too, and offered to keep him safe if she ever needed him to. "You didn't tell anyone else about this, did you?" I asked. Pieces of the puzzle were starting to fit together. Did this vamp coven, Sanguine Sanctum, have something to do with Stef's mom's disappearance? Did they have this monster kill my dad? *Who else could it be?*

I stepped closer to him and handed the notebook back, holding his wrist for a second. He looked down at my hand

and then back at me.

"No, no one. Abraxas suspects something, but he didn't press for more information when I refused to talk. All I said was that my mom wrote his name down as a contact in case something happened to her and told me to go to him for help."

"Excellent cover story. Believable and leaves out the details of how your mom went missing. Smart."

"My momma didn't raise no fool." He scrunched up his nose. "Or is it *a* fool?"

I couldn't help but laugh. "Well, I'll be damned! Banshee Boy has a touch of humor."

"Only on rare occasions." He had the cheesiest grin on his face.

"Ha! I like you. I think we'll continue to get along just fine." I patted him on the shoulder and motioned for him to follow me to the front desks.

"Cool. I'm excited. So like friends? I don't have many of those, obviously."

I nodded. "Yes, definitely friends and coworkers."

"Outstanding. This is what real people do. I love my mom, but I hated being alone most of the time. I always wished I had gone to school or something and made some friends."

"I bet. She should have loosened that grip a little. Plenty of Sups to make friends with. Being cooped up all your life has a tendency to limit your circle, but it's not a bad thing if you ask me."

"What makes you say that?"

He had a puzzled look on his face. Man, if he only knew how bad public education was for the Sups. It was challenging trying to blend in with society. Even an ounce of supernatural in the blood spelled disaster.

"Trust me, I attended to public school with a bunch of Unsups. Nothing but backstabbing, drama-filled assholes, if you ask me."

"Sounds rough."

"Oh, it was. Not being able to tell people about my dad's real job, what I was learning to do. I had to hide a big part of myself from people I loved. Mostly I hated lying."

"I guess that makes sense with supernatural bounties, hunting, and all. Keeping it secret."

"Yes. He warned me to tell no one at school who I was. We lived a half-lie, and I hated it. Still do, so I don't make close friends with other humans. I stick to the Sups. Easier that way. Well, in some ways." Memories invaded my headspace. My ex-girlfriend and I tried normal together. Didn't work out, and she crushed my heart when she turned on me.

"I don't know if it helps, but it sounds like it beats being cooped up in a mansion your entire life."

"Ha! Sort of." Stef had a point there, and I had Abraxas now. But even then, I worried, did I really? I had to find my dad's killers and sometimes I wondered if Brax was a distraction. *A pretty hot and tempting one too.* I'd find out soon enough if that was true enough.

"So, what do we do next?" he asked me.

"Let's start a case file and get a board set up." I walked over to the wall and flipped it around to reveal a chalkboard. "I want you to feel prepared before we gather intel. Remember, spectral form only, keep to the shadows when possible, and stay out of crowded areas. Things like that."

"Okay. Sneaking around should be easy enough."

"I need to see if I can find a floor plan for their compound."

"Where would you get details like that?"

"Abraxas, and he always comes through for me." I picked a piece of chalk up and jotted down what we knew about the case so far.

"You really trust that demon?"

"I do, why?"

"I always thought demons were untrustworthy."

"No. They keep their word, but they are tricky, and that is where you'll run into issues. Oh, and never sign a contract with them."

"Oh. Do you think Abraxas will trick or mislead you?"

"No, he isn't like the others. Brax prefers to stay neutral. He likes to keep a balance; much like my dad did."

"You're right. I shouldn't question you."

"No! I like you questioning my choices, even if you're the assistant. Don't be afraid to speak up. I am not perfect. We should work together on everything. Keeps me from going overboard."

"Are you sure?" his brows furrowed.

"Yes. This is what I am thinking. I'll head to Club Inferno while you stay here and continue sorting through the cases. Get all those papers and folders on the table put away in the basement area I showed you last night in case something happens. "

"In case of what?"

"Honestly, I think we might have someone after the both of us. It's probably those vamps. Think about what happened. They wanted your mom for something and my dad gone–I'm sure of it. My skin is prickling all over. My sixth sense is telling me it's them. Camping out downstairs is your safest bet. No one knows about the basement, not even Brax."

"Before I head on out, does this look right?"

I pointed to the chalkboard where I had written about

my dad's death and his mom's disappearance. I drew lines to the monster with the vamp coven underneath circled with a question mark.

"Looks good. You can add my mom's name instead of Stef's mom."

"Of course. You haven't mentioned it yet. Come and write it down for me here." I handed the chalk over.

"Clíodhna." He whispered while writing it on the board.

I added what I needed to do next. *Visit Abraxas.*

Stef's eyebrow raised, and his lips tightened. "Are you sure he can help us?"

"Yes." I flipped the board around, watching it slide back into the wall.

"Okay."

"Fenris, stay here with Stef." Fenris rushed up to my face, putting his front paws on my chest as he glared into my eyes. "You will sense what's coming before he does. Please do this for me."

He snarled before licking my cheek and sitting next to Stef, who immediately flinched. I chuckled a little and smiled.

"Remember, he doesn't bite people he likes. And don't be afraid to talk to him. He's cool."

Stef nodded his head and continued to work — Fenris at his side. I grabbed my wallet and small flip phone, and stuffed both in my pockets. I pulled my jacket off the rack near the door and looked back. They'd be okay. Plus, I needed a break, and Brax's delicious face was calling my name.

CHAPTER FIVE

INTERRUPTION

Aaima

I headed to Brax's club on my favorite mode of transportation: my motorcycle. The afternoon sun blazed down on me, but the wind whipped around me and kept me cool. The air was full of possibility, the smell of gasoline and freedom. I revved the engine and sped up, the vibrations of the engine coursing through me like I was part of the machine.

I reveled in the thrill of being out on the open road, taking in the sights and sounds of the city. As I weaved my way closer to the club. Trees and buildings blurred around me, transforming into a kaleidoscope of color in motion.

The black painted bricks of Club Inferno came into view. The blue neon sign was so bright that it stood out even in the daylight. My stomach fluttered and my heart thudded hard against my chest. Brax had always been a dangerous man, but he hadn't failed me yet.

I pulled past the entrance and careened into the employee parking lot. Lights inside the club weren't on yet, and it looked dead besides a few employees getting ready for their shifts. Everyone there knew who I was. Bethany waved while the others continued to work, taking in supplies for the restaurant on the ground floor.

"Hey! How's it going?" I jogged to her side and picked up a box, following her inside.

"Oh, you know the usual B.S. you coming by tonight for some drinks? I'll make your favorite." she winked.

The prospect of a drink was mighty tempting, but I knew I had to decline. "I'm back to work. Maybe another time?"

Bethany stopped in her tracks. "Oh wow, I didn't know. How long you planning to visit the boss this afternoon? I'll be manning the bar in the restaurant until Vexx gets here."

"First day back. I didn't tell anyone. If I think I have time, I'll stop and grab something so we can chat a minute. I'm surprised Vexx is back so soon. How's that little one of hers?" Beth and Vexx had been friends of mine for years. We knew each other since high school. They had checked in on me almost every day since dad's death. I knew they always had my back if some shit went sideways while I was at the club.

"Doing good. If we don't see you today, we both work the rest of the week."

"I'll see what I can arrange."

"Or you could answer a text or two instead."

"Yeah, I'll work on it. Catch ya later promise." Those two were texting fools. I didn't enjoy clicking through each number to get to the letter I wanted. Still, I needed to reach out to both of them. I couldn't afford to lose allies, let alone friends.

I entered the area with the bar's supplies and food, walking past the kitchens to a set of stairs leading up to Brax's office on the second floor. Stationed at the top of the stairs were his two bodyguards. They looked like gargoyle statues perched in perfect silence, their expressions cold and unreadable.

I had encountered them many times before, but that didn't make them any less intimidating. Their presence reminded me I was entering a place where power was held and secrets were kept. It was like stepping into a whole different world.

"Is he busy?" I asked.

The guard named Ronan answered me. "If it's you, you can go in no matter what."

"Thanks."

Staring up at them, I had the feeling they weren't thrilled about me being there. Ronan looked like he wanted to say something more, but held his tongue instead. Braun never uttered a single word the entire time. His eyes followed my every move, though.

Each of them was nearly seven feet tall, their bodies built

like mountains. Both had shaved heads and were identical twins, but Braun had a thick beard and mustache. Ronan remained clean shaven. As demons, they had few physical differences from humans unless they wanted to show their true selves off. When they did, both donned twisting horns and eyes that glowed orange.

Even though they knew I was on Abraxas's side, they still looked at me with an air of distrust, and I knew why. I had sent more than a couple of their kind packing in my time.

I swallowed hard and made my way up the stairs past them. My heart pounding in anticipation. I felt a slight breeze roll past me. As big as Braun was, he had snuck by and hurried in front to open the door to Brax's office. He escorted me in. The clicking sound of the door closing echoed in my ears.

Abraxas sat at his desk amidst towering piles of paperwork.

"Damn! Jackpot on souls, I see," I said.

He looked up quickly, his eyes twinkling. "Wow, a visit so soon?" He bit his lower lip, and a spark flew between us. Brax glanced up again. "You're here on business, not pleasure?"

“That depends.” I grinned.

His brow raised inquisitively. “Depends on what?” his sapphire gaze fixed right on me.

“What you do next.” I sat down on the couch across from him and waited to see what he’d do. My entire body burned with desire. Abraxas was tall and muscular. With a face that could melt the hardest heart–a chiseled jawline, honey blonde hair, and those piercing blue eyes that seemed to swallow me up whenever I looked into them.

I smirked as he shifted in his seat and squirmed. We rarely saw each other in a sober state. This encounter would be a test of our feelings for each other. Neither of us had expected to go beyond the friends-with-benefits stage. But something changed between us.

I remembered that night in the VIP section. I was hooking up with Scarlett again. Gods! She was divine, from her plump lips to her thick thighs and round tits. It hadn’t been the first time we slept together with Brax joining in. But this time, something was off. I couldn’t figure out why he got up and left right in the middle of our weekly tryst. Scar and I had barely started. Then it clicked—he wanted something more, he wanted only me.

We had been getting closer for a while and I knew we were playing a dangerous game. I was a hunter; Brax was a demon, but I didn't care. I had never stopped a good fuck before, but I dropped Scarlett like a bag of rocks and raced after him. Left poor Scar half naked with the curtains pulled wide open. *Whoops!*

We never agreed to exclusivity, but he didn't talk to me for a week. That was one of the worst weeks of my life. I craved Abraxas and everything about him, no one else mattered. Truth was, it was easy to cut Scarlett loose.

I looked up at Brax and waited for him to make a move. He strolled over to me and peered down at me with his deep eyes. He brushed his lips against mine, his fingers caressing my sides, sending sparks through my entire body. His strong hands moved from my waist up to cup my face as he kissed me deeper. As he pulled away, I tugged at his button-up shirt.

The deep crimson red of it engulfed my vison. All I wanted was more–more of his touch, his kiss, more of him.

"This is unfamiliar territory," he finally spoke.

"And?" I replied, looking up at him. His gaze was intense and his words had been a question in search of an answer.

Brax took my hands in his. "What is it you want from me?" He sat on the couch right beside me and turned. His fingers gliding up my stomach to the center of my chest where my heart lay beating faster at his proximity closing in on me.

My eyes focused on his. "You know what I want." I whispered, running my fingers through my newly dyed teal hair, trying to tease him a little more.

His gaze intensified as he leaned over to get even closer, our faces almost touching. "I like the new color. Teal is my favorite." Brax spoke in a low whisper that sent shivers down my spine.

My cheeks flushed, and I smiled at his compliment. "Thanks."

I could feel his breath on my skin when he said, "I want

you. All of you. I'd burn down the world if it meant you were mine."

My heart raced. "Thought I was yours already." I murmured softly into his ear.

I pulled him close and planted a kiss on his lips. His tongue twirled with mine as his hands embraced my torso. He lifted me up effortlessly and placed me on his lap. Our lower halves locked together–revealing he was hard as a rock. My arms roped arms around his neck as his face dug into my chest. His hands slid up my waist, pulling my shirt right off. "Mmmm, I've always liked your no bra policy," Brax whispered as he took one of my nipples into his mouth.

I swayed against his body. The desire to experience all of him increased as his fingers trailed down my waistline until they rested at the opening of my leather pants. A moan escaped my lips as my breathing grew quick and shallow, my heart rate rising with each passing second.

Then there was a loud knock at the door. "One moment!" Brax shouted.

Both of us still grinding hard against each other. "Son of a—" I groaned.

"I know. Your lips, your everything," he sighed.

"Same, Brax. Same." I touched my fingers to his lips.

"For a moment, I thought you weren't sure," he whispered.

"No, I crave you and only you."

The knocking began again, louder than before. He barked out an angry response on the other side of the door. "I said a damn moment!" He stood up, still holding me close, with my legs wrapped around his waist. I didn't want to let go. Brax sat me down gently on the couch, fixed himself, and cracked the door open. "What the hell, Braun?"

"Sir, I apologize, but this is urgent." I took a peek at Braun from the slight opening in the doorway. His complexion was pale as a ghost as his chest heaved up and down from running up the stairs.

"This better be a bloody emergency or else," Brax snarled. "I was in the middle of an important meeting with the Direwolf Bounty hunter Agency."

"Again, I'm sorry, but it's Mammon."

He swore under his breath. "Shit. Tell her I'm coming right away."

"Will do, sir."

Brax closed the door and faced me. "I hate to cut this short, but something has come up involving the Infernal Council."

I sighed. "Damn, serious matters then? What's the council again? I guess I'll have to get you next time."

"The council I am on is considered Hell's most esteemed organization. We can discuss more later. Did you need anything? Besides..."

"Yes, actually I came here looking for floor plans for Sanguine Sanctum's, compound. Do you have a way to get those for me?"

"What? Why? What do you need them for?"

"I'm investigating a lead, but I can't talk about it here."

Brax nodded, then came up and kissed my forehead, and I instinctively reached out and hugged him to my body. He whispered in my ear, "I could get used to this."

"Me too." I nuzzled my face into his chest.

Another knock came, and Braun opened the door.

"An important meeting, huh?" he said, with one eyebrow raised up.

Brax motioned for him to leave with a look that could kill on his face.

"Yes, important. She's just leaving."

"Understood." Braun cowered before Brax. He was bulkier and even a smidge taller, but Abraxas wasn't a lower-level demon whelp, and looks were deceiving. He could have torn him to bits in minutes.

"Leave now. I'll be there shortly. You can tell Mammon I had a meeting, top priority. Leave it at that or I'll have your throat."

"Sir! Yes, sir!" Braun quickly shut the door and disappeared down the hallway. I could hear him bounding down the corridor to get the message to this Mammon. I'd have to ask about that later. Brax broke me from my thoughts. "Now, back to your inquiry. I will see what I can do. Just don't mention this to anyone else."

"Zipped lips. You know how I work."

"I do. I don't trust many Sups and Victor is definitely up to something." his eyes darkened and his face hardened. He gazed into my eyes, waiting for my response. I stared back and shook my head. He kissed me again.

"Tell me everything later?" I asked.

"Yes, can't tell you here. I am going to assume Mammon is directly downstairs in the restaurant area, and she hates when I aid either side and that I prefer staying neutral. Not that there are sides, but she thinks so. If only she could see the gray in each situation. She's also prone to eavesdropping and has tried to bug the place multiple times."

"Would you be able to stop by DBA later?"

"Yes."

"Tonight then?"

"Yes, I'll reach out to my inside contact and get back to you." His eyes continuously scanned the room, and then they locked on the door. For just a second, I swore I saw flames around his irises. "I need to get going. I hate to cut this short."

"Same. Later? You and me?"

"Tonight. I promise."

He kissed me again before leaving his office. Damn, what a bust. I didn't get laid or find any information to help me with the vamp situation. On the plus side, I got to see how Brax really felt. I shivered all over, thinking about that last kiss and how he held me. I hadn't felt this strongly in years, but now my emotions were even more intense than before.

Enough with the mush. Concentrate. Something about this Mammon character seemed off. Should I stick around longer and try to listen in on them? I knew all the hiding spots in Brax's office. *Or do I leave the way I came in?* Demons weren't vamps, so there was no chance they'd smell me, but they had heightened hearing. I wasn't sure I wanted to risk interfering by trying to scope things out without Brax's permission.

I looked around his office, tidied the couch, and headed out when Braun slipped in again.

"Damn, I'm leaving, okay? Sheesh." I tried to walk out the

door, but he closed it faster than I could get out. He was huge compared to little ol' me. I glared up at him, expressionless. He would not intimidate me. We stared at each other, the silence between us thick with anticipation. "I said I was leaving, Braun."

He leaned over to my ear and whispered after I tried the knob. "You need to go out the window."

"What? Why? It's a two-story drop."

"Oh, please! You're Assad's daughter, don't play coy with me. I know you can jump from this height without issues. You got lucky when your family got touched by the Sup. Now, please trust me."

"You've hardly spoken a damn word to me, and you expect me—"

Braun covered my mouth and put his index finger against my lips, cutting me off mid-sentence. He motioned to the window and directed me there himself. His caution shocked me. I looked at him again, whispering, "What's going on? What's the big deal?"

His shoulders fell a bit, and he mumbled, “Mammon, she’s a tricky bitch. I’m sorry I’m distant. My duty is to protect him at all costs. I promised his father I’d keep him safe. Shit... I hear their footsteps.”

I simply nodded in response. He had never been this way, and I feared for Brax.

“Please keep him safe for me.” I breathed out.

He gave a sharp jerk of his head in response. The sound of voices coming from the hallway caught both our attention. Braun whipped the window open, and I crawled out on the ledge as he closed it. I had half a mind to hang there for a moment to see if I could hear anything. But thought better of it and leapt down to the ground. My feet met the pavement sending a hard jolt throughout my body. I dashed out of the alley and jogged straight for my bike.

Instinctively, I wanted to hop on, hit the clutch, and get going. Instead, I rolled the bike down half a block before starting it. Not only did I leave with nothing, but now I worried about Abraxas and the mess he could be in.

The whole thing ignited my intuition. My skin felt like it was being pricked by a ton of needles again. Whoever this Mammon character was. Something more had to be going on than what Brax had told me. I hoped he'd tell me later exactly what. In the meantime, I had to trust that Brax, Braun, and Ronan could handle the situation.

Chapter Six

Succubus Bitch

Abraxas

My gaze lingered on Aaima's piercing green eyes as I stepped closer, crushing my lips against hers. Fire spread through my veins as her delicate lashes brushed my skin. I wished I could remain there and freeze time, so I wouldn't have to meet the looming obligations that awaited me.

Mammon had failed to warn me of her visit. I wasn't sure if it was a formal matter for the Infernal Council or some darker agenda. I was betting on the latter since she had pilfered one of my sacred amulets. It didn't leave me completely immobilized, but my strength and power were not at their peak.

Gnashing my teeth, I steeled myself for the confrontation ahead. It infuriated me to know that Mammon belonged to the council now. So, I'd greet that succubus witch out of ceremony, nothing more.

Mammon thought her newfound position gave her license to trample on her fellow demons. The council had elevated her to my rank. And she didn't hesitate to flaunt it every time we crossed paths. Ronan remained at the end of the hallway, his feet firmly planted at the top of the staircase, while Braun went back into my office to get Aaima out–somehow.

I knew Mammon had no clue that my heart belonged to Aaima. But if she ever found out, she'd use it against me in an instant. I refused to let the woman I loved get mixed up with that succubus. Mammon slinked up the stairs and tried to hold my arm, but I declined, gently bowing away from her touch.

"Greetings, fellow council member. Please state your business." I ground my teeth and mustered a smile.

"Abraxas, darling, I need your help." she fluttered her eyelids and inched closer. I clenched my jaw and pushed away, my hands motioning her further down the hall.

Ronan stepped forward and led her with an iron grip at her waist. "This way, please," he commanded, his steps quickening as they reached my office.

"Yes, all meetings need to be held privately in my quarters." I forged ahead deliberately, slowing to a snail's pace. Braun had yet to emerge, which meant my girl was giving him hell. I'd never expect less from Aaima.

She would soon figure out something was wrong. I longed to tell her more, but Mammon kept all her dealings shrouded in secrecy. I pinned my hopes on the succubus coming to me for aid, giving me a chance to outwit her. I had a plan to convince her to return my amulet, thus freeing me from her grasp.

I scanned the door to my office as we approached it. Still no sight of Braun. I stalled and turned to face the wench. "Before we begin, is there anything you'd want to eat or drink during our meeting? I can send for it right away." but Mammon clicked her heels and leapt for the door. She swung it open, revealing Braun standing by the window. His gaze locked on her and he observed her every move.

"Why, hello there, Braun? A pleasure seeing you, as always," she crooned as she careened over to him.

Braun grunted in response. His stance was rigid, and when she took a step toward him, he lurched away, taking a step backwards. Her hand reached out to touch him, but he shifted out of her reach.

Braun remained tensed as her face scrunched up in a pout. "Doesn't talk much, does he?" She marched back in my direction, then boldly sat down on the couch. Her hands glided up her leg, meeting the hem of the tight ivory dress she wore. Trying to allure me with her seductive powers. An undeniable urge filled the room. Braun and Ronan licked their lips and strode over to her. Both caressed every inch of her body as her lips curled up in a devious smile. “Now that’s more like it. Won’t you join us?” her finger beckoned, but I did not respond.

I barked orders at my guards. “Leave now.” My words filled with power as the sheer force broke the hold she had on them. Ronan remained stoic, but Braun’s face filled with anger. I didn’t need these two mucking things up. “I said to go now. I’ll deal with you both later.” Before I continued to exert my power and stifle hers. Her fingers twirled in the air. I could barely make out the blueish-silver smokey threads flowing through the air. As they swirled around me, I caught a faint whiff of their sweet fragrance and felt their cool touch on my skin before dissipating.

I scoffed at her. “Forget it–I won’t be falling for your tricks.” Mammon was a powerful succubus, but her charms would not work on me. Her abilities could never compete with the feelings Aaima gave me when she entered the same room.

“Too bad. I like a bit of pleasure with my business.”

"I don't. What do you want?"

"I heard whispers you may know something about Sayyaads."

"What? Who told you that?" I roared, wondering who had the nerve to tell her about them. Once she found out they were long gone, she'd probably torture the poor soul to bits.

Supposedly, the Sayyaads were an ancient race of Sups, but they seemed more like mythical nonsense to me. Despite my father regaling me with tales of their battles in my youth.

Mammon didn't back down. She crossed her arms. Her grave expression intensified as she continued. "I've heard they still exist, but have gone into hiding. You're neutral, like your dad was before you. I thought maybe he helped hide a few of them away somewhere. Don't you have his records here?"

"My father told me stories about them when I was a child, but nothing else. Sayyaads are more like supernatural bedtime stories told to us to keep us from exposing our world to the humans." I noted the flash of disappointment on her face but finished my sentence, "And if they existed, they're all dead now. I can't help you. This is inexplicable, even for you. Go after something plausible next time."

"Lies. I know you have sources. Ask them to look around. What about the daughter of the late Assad? The bounty hunter. Whatever her name is."

"First, relinquish my amulet and I'll see what I can dig up for you. Second, hire the DBA yourself. It's not like you're unable to locate the information to do so." I regretted what I said right away. Aaima didn't need to be intertwined with the demon clans.

"No, I want concrete facts. Rumors have been floating around that we may have one in our little city here. I want evidence you found one or have knowledge of their presence, and it better be soon." Her fists slammed into the couch.

"I haven't heard these rumors? Who's your informant?" I demanded.

"Once you give me what I need, I'll reveal my source. I also need leverage from the demon side and, well, honey, you're it."

"Never call me that again." My expression contorted with repugnance.

Mammon sprang off the couch. Her countenance a breath away from mine. "Soon enough, you'll be on my side. You'll see." The tip of her nose touched mine, making my skin crawl. Something about her was off and I had my fair share of dealings with other succubi.

She pushed the boundaries more than any other demon I knew. "I am on no one's side." I told her.

"Not true. You pretend you're keeping the balance, but you still hold a bias. Like right now. I'm a dirty succubus, right?"

"That's not true." I responded.

"You're lying!" she hissed.

"No, you're a petty thief and I want my property back." Fury built up inside me. She made assumptions about my character I didn't like. I held everyone in the same regard until they showed me otherwise.

"Find me something on the Sayyaads, then. Do it now." Her voice quivered in desperation.

"Fool's errand, but whatever you want, I suppose."

"Good. I'll check up on you later today." Her index finger jabbed right into the center of my chest.

"Check back in a week. This isn't some rushed endeavor, you twit." I seized her wrist and held tight, leading her arm down to her side before letting go.

"I'll check in whenever I feel like it." She stomped her heels on the floor.

I chuckled, "What, are you a toddler?"

Her eyes blazed wild with hate, and her aura smoldered with rage. "Don't fuck with me Abraxas, you'll regret it." Mammon's eyes gleamed cobalt blue and remained illuminated as her energy mounted. A powerful wave exploded from her and swept over me. Sending my head reeling back. After regaining myself, I returned her gaze without flinching.

"Are we done here?" I asked before I stepped behind my desk, putting distance between us.

"For now. You want your precious little amulet back? You'll give me what I want or find something close to it."

"Fine, we'll do it your way," I said without hesitation. I had no other choice—the amulet was too important for me to abandon.

Mammon smirked. She gave me one solid once over before prying the door open. "A shame you didn't want to. I would have rocked your world and then some." She said, as Braun stepped in.

"Doubt it."

Ronan escorted her out, and Braun stayed. When their footsteps become nothing but a whisper, he spoke, "That was close. I got Aaima out the window before that witch shot in here like she owns the place. How did she steal one of your amulets?"

"I don't know. That's what I've been trying to figure out. I also don't understand this goose chase she's sending me on. The Sayyaads all died in the Great Extermination, well, according to my father's records, anyway."

"Give her what you have and be done with this mess. You can't afford to get tangled up with that succubus."

"I wish things were that simple. Only a desperate soul would seek something that doesn't exist anymore. I'm not sure she'll give it back even if I show my father's records to her. There's more to this than meets the eye. What we need to figure out is why she needs a Sayyaad."

"Are you going to ask Aaima for help with this? She'd be capable of getting your amulet back while you distract Mammon."

Braun's idea was terrible. "No, I don't want that succubus near her."

"Scared of what might happen between them?" he asked.

"No. Maybe. I don't know if Aaima has faced a succubus demon before. I am opposed to her going in unprepared." Braun knew how to get under my skin. He walked a fine line talking to me like that. Even with one amulet missing, I could tear his throat out.

"Or you don't want to find the woman you love being screwed by the demon you hate most right now."

"That too. Thank you for bringing it up. You need to watch

your mouth and remember who's in charge."

"What?" Braun shrugged.

I cleared my throat. Braun wanted me to admit I had become the jealous type, and by hells, I had. I hadn't found myself in the position of loving someone so deeply before. The territory was new to me, and I didn't want to fuck it up and lose her. I had lost so much already.

"Sir, if I may be so bold. I can tell Aaima loves you. You shouldn't worry. I'm sure she can handle one tiny succubus."

"Too bold." I grabbed him by the shirt and lifted him off the ground.

"Sorry, sir. I'll comb over the club twice for bugs," he eked out.

"Good. Go now." I ordered as I let go. His feet falling back down on the floor.

I sat down in my chair. *Aaima loves me?* Deep down, I hoped he was right.

Chapter Seven

Hunter's Stew

Aaima

As soon as I hopped on the bike, I changed my plan and headed to John's house. He had to have some answers for me. I made my way to the outskirts of the city. The breeze whipped through my jacket and tickled up my spine. The concrete paths and tall buildings disappeared, giving way to fields and trees. John was smart for living outside the city. All the stress and chaos rushed out of my limbs. The sweet scent of fresh air filled my nostrils.

I kept my eyes peeled for the old rusty sign that signaled where I needed to turn. You had to be careful, or you'd miss it. I slowed down and hit my blinker on. I turned onto an unpaved road and drove slowly down the path. Half a mile up was a large oak tree. I parked near it and trekked on foot the rest of the way up to his place.

Talismans for protection hung from several pine trees. Some of their symbols I was unfamiliar with. A railed wood fence with sturdy wire wrapped around the cabin, enclosing a garden with trellises of squash and tomatoes vines. Smoke puffed out of the chimney. I hopped across the stone path leading to the door. It was colder out here than in the city, so I tucked my hands in my pockets to warm them.

I looked at my phone when I got to the steps. The time read five fifteen, and the sun was rapidly setting. *It will be dark soon*. I knew better than to stand there waiting and knocked hard on the door. I leaned my body to the right and tried to peer through the window.

The curtains blocked just enough of the inside that I

couldn't make anything out, though I was pretty sure I heard someone's feet shuffling to the door. That someone had to be John, but I questioned it for a second, calling out, "John, it's me! You home?"

I went on the defense just in case. John and my dad had been partners for years before John retired, so I wasn't sure what to expect. I hadn't been to his cabin in several years.

I pulled my knife out from under the cuff of my boot and gripped it tight. I watched as a shadow emerged near the window and briefly scanned the woods behind me.

John opened the door, peeked his head out, grabbed me by the arm, and rushed me in. "What are you doing out here? Are you crazy? It's almost dark?"

"I need help with some clues my dad left me."

He looked down to see I still had my knife. "Put that damn thing away." he flicked his hands at me.

I nodded and tucked it back into my boot. "Sorry, I was just being cautious. I don't think any of us associated with the DBA on the Sup side are safe right now."

His lips pursed together as a faint yes escaped from his mouth. "I reckon you're right. Here, come join me. I've baked bread, and I'm working up some hunter's stew." He walked over to the old wooden stove and stirred a large black pot with a ladle resting on the counter nearby.

"You know I am always up for hunter's stew." I joined him by his side.

I stood by his handcrafted table, glancing around. It had been a few years since I had been here last. My dad and John worked on different hunts together. Dad had begged me to come out here more often, and I refused. It brought up memories that tugged at my heart.

"Ah, I see you're looking around. Been five years since you stepped in here last."

"Yeah, nothing has changed. Everything's still the same."

"It's the only place with familiarity for me and I like it. Gives me peace." he smiled, continuing to stir.

"Damn. Ain't that the truth, though? After the bounties you worked with dad, I'm sure it was nice to come home to your own space away from all of that."

"You settled down into your apartment just fine. Same thing, right?" he asked.

"No, it doesn't feel like home. Home is when mom was still around."

"Still pains me today. Isabelle knew your dad could take that hit, but her love outweighed her smarts that evening."

"Something tells me it wasn't just her love, John. She was human with some witch in the mix. My dad wasn't."

"Yeah 'bout that."

"You knew about him, didn't you? Why didn't you say anything to me the other day?"

"I did. He told me right before the night he died, but your mom wasn't half human, like she claimed. She was fully a witch, but hid it from folks for good reason."

"Hmm... so, what else did he tell you? I can accept that my mom was a witch. That alone explains all the magic she knew and tried to teach me. But my dad's journal said he was two hundred years old! No human can live that long."

John sighed deeply, filled two bowls with stew, and sat them on the table. He raked his fingers through his beard. He looked sad and beaten down. Wrinkles dappled the corner of his eyelids, making the creases in his forehead appear more pronounced. His eyes told more stories than most, too. You could tell just by looking at them he had seen terrible things. My stomach sank.

"John..."

"Let me get some spoons and bread for this. Let's eat, and then we'll talk."

"I'll help." I said, taking two cups off hooks and filling them with tea from a pot on the stove. John sat our bowls down and sliced the bread. Moments like these were simple, but precious to me. Knowing what existed out there created a deep appreciation for the mundane.

I went to my seat and sat down, shifted around trying to get comfortable. John walked over to his cabinet area, opened a drawer, pulled out two large spoons, and handed one to me. He sat down and smiled at me.

John had always been the best cook. I was excited to dig into a home-cooked meal for once. I loved everything he made. Dad couldn't cook worth a damn. He tried but failed miserably. I had the best memories of camping with our hunter friends.

I always thought the ones who had a small amount of Sup power were still human. Dad made it sound like we weren't even human. I hoped John knew what I really was.

He sat down and placed the bread board between us. He took a small sip of stew and motioned for me to eat. I wasted no time digging in. The flavors of potatoes, venison, carrots, and herbs hit my mouth and I couldn't help but scarf down the entire bowl in minutes. I teared up a little when the last spoonful left my lips. We would never go camping together again, or make Hunter's Stew as a family.

John and dad would argue about what to put in it. John always won out, thank goodness. Maybe when the dust settled, we could go on our annual trip, but bring Steph with and form new traditions. I had the feeling John would like him.

The thought made me happy and sad all at the same time. I missed my dad, despite the things he kept from me.

"What else did you find in your dad's journals?" John asked.

"I thought we were only Sup-touched. You know, humans with a bit of supernatural DNA so what was he? What am I? What did he need to tell me?"

"Your dad hid a lot of things from people, Aaima, and he did it to protect you and your mom."

"But my mom knew, right?"

"Yes, he told me that much. She knew that if he died, you wouldn't have a chance in hell to survive. I tried to convince him to let me take the reins on that last case. He swore it'd be easy and here we are without him." His brow furrowed before he tucked his head down. "I'm sorry it's me talking to you about this and not your dad."

"Don't say that."

His face filled with pain and sadness. His hands shook,

clinking the bowl with his spoon. "Damn you, Assad," he whispered under his breath.

"John..." this was not like him at all. He was shaking.

"Sorry, he was my best friend. He was like a brother to me. I'd be dead too if it wasn't for him. Truth is, I'm struggling. He knew things about Sups that others don't. There were secrets he shared with me, but there was so much more, and now we're both left in the dark."

His shoulders slumped, and he buried his chin down toward his chest. I flew out of my chair and stood next to him. I slowly put my hand on his shoulder, hoping he'd receive it well. His right arm crossed his chest, and he placed his large hand over mine, whispering, "Thanks." I patted his shoulder in response and stayed still.

Several long moments of silence passed. We stayed like that for a bit. It had been long enough that the stew grew cold. I added more to both our bowls to even out the temperature and buttered more bread slices before standing next to him again. I had been selfish. Regret weighed heavy on my heart. If

I had given the situation more thought, I know the outcome would have been different.

"I'm sorry for being so stupid. I'm sure if I wasn't off being rebellious, dad wouldn't be dead," I mumbled.

"Eh, you're still young. Your dad and I, we were like that. Hell, I took to the drink more than he did. He quit, and I didn't. He quit for you."

We stayed still for several minutes longer. My hand on his shoulder and his hand cupped over mine. We hadn't mourned together. I hadn't given him the chance, and the guilt I felt weighed down my entire body.

"I know I messed up, and I'm still apologizing for my actions."

"Don't." He spoke the words with a force I hadn't heard before. "I was young and dumb, too. I don't think I came into my own until my thirties. All I have to say is don't dwell on the things you did or didn't do. You just move on and do better, ya' hear?"

I closed my eyes and shook my head before I settled into the chair across from him again. John wiped at his eyes and sat up straight.

We ate our food. One slow bite after another. I savored each mouthful. Each morsel stirred my memories. I had been lucky. Yes, I grew up in a life most Unsups would find terrifying, but my parents, and John, made it worthwhile. Maybe some hunters learned to experience life to the fullest. After all, we knew what was out there and didn't let the truth change how we lived. We didn't sit on doing the right thing—we *did* it. Hunters didn't wait for fortune to find them. They went after it because most understood life is cruel. At any moment, life could take away what we held dear. Some knew this pain better than others.

In the back of my mind, I had known the dangers, but I held onto the belief that my dad was near invincible. I was wrong, of course. The last few months had shown me the errors of my ways. I needed to embrace each moment of joy and savor it. Much like each bite of stew.

"Now, back to this business with your dad and his secrets."

John sighed.

I rested my elbows on the table while waiting for his answers. "What was he? What am I?"

"We know there are humans who have a smidgen of the supernatural in their DNA and their talents and strengths vary, but your dad told me he wasn't even human."

"Then what was he?"

"He called himself a Sayyaad. He said Sayyaads were a race of supernatural beings that kept the peace. Mother Nature's way of keeping balance. But creatures like vamps and others hunted them down to near extinction. Your people were like the equalizers of the supernatural community, so their powers easily matched the fiercest of creatures. All the stories are true. Demons roamed the deserts, and vampires were out of control. Werewolves dined on the people in the forests, and ghosts could haunt a person into an early grave. He even speculated that the gods and goddesses were here once, too." He paused, waiting for me to respond. Or maybe he was trying to read my reaction. When I didn't, John continued.

"The Sayyaads cleaned up the mess and kept the paranormal safe. Until the vampires wanted to rule over humans."

"Sayyaad," I mumbled under my breath.

"Yes, and that's all he told me. He also said the tribes had dwindled, and his family was one of the few that survived. He told me to tell you to go home and look for more answers. Go to the family cabin and start there first."

I sighed. That was it? What was he so afraid to tell John, his best friend? My frustration grew. All he left me with were those stupid journals and stale bread crumbs. "I thought he sold the cabin years ago?"

"Your dad lied about selling it, even faked the papers to leave a false trail. He wanted to protect the place for you to have later. He told me I couldn't share more than that with you. All the answers are there if something should happen to him, he said." Sadness lingered on his face.

"That's it? I go to the family cabin, and I'll find all the answers?"

"As far as I know, yes."

"This is utter bullshit." I slammed my fist on the table. "Why didn't he tell me sooner? Why did he keep this from me?" I raised my voice, my body tense with anger.

All my life, he hid this from me and barely told John anything. The one person besides my mom that he trusted with his life. Dad knew how much the cabin meant to me and he lied. I mourned the loss for years. All my memories of mom took place there and in an instant he had taken them from me. I remembered coming home from school and him breaking the news to me. It devastated me.

How could he do that? Confusion turned into rage within me. "He trusted you with his life, but not with this? Not with the truth of what he was? He lied to me about the cabin. He knew how upset I was!"

"Aaima." John's voice stayed calm. I didn't get it. My dad kept this large part of himself hidden from his best friend and me, his only daughter.

"Your dad had his reasons, and he was oath-bound."

"Screw his oaths and secrets," I spat out.

"Hey now, that's not fair. Your dad promised your grandad that he'd keep the family secret."

"Fair to who? Surely not you or me. Keeping secrets hurts people in the long run. Even when the person thinks they're sparing someone from hurt and pain. The lie breaks trust and it's difficult to repair. How am I supposed to trust anything he's told you?"

"Hold up a sec. This is your father we're talking about. He was a good man."

John sat his spoon down and gave me his full attention, but I needed fresh air. I stood up and headed for the front door. He told my mom, but maybe because they had me? But he didn't tell John everything, and this worried me. What was a Sayyaad and why did he keep it a secret?

"I need some damn air." My fingers gripped the knob tight. I opened it and walked out to the porch.

I didn't understand the need for all this secrecy. Did dad think he was invincible? Why he hadn't told me sooner? I wasn't a teenager anymore. I took in the night air and tried to calm my senses.

John edged out the front door a few minutes later and stood next to me in silence.

"You're allowed to be pissed," he finally said.

"Damn right I am! Someone, something is still after me, and I am ill-prepared." I turned to him with my fists balled up.

"Don't take it out on old uncle John now." He chuckled.

I looked down and released my hands. My fingers dangled at my sides.

"Sorry, it's just... all I have is half-assed answers and more questions I don't know what to do with. Frustration doesn't even begin to cover it."

"Your dad should have told both of us sooner. He said you had Fenris, and that would be enough to protect you."

"What? Fenris and I almost died!"

"I know. I am sure he does too and regrets his actions."

"John, my dad's dead."

"Hey now, don't say it like that."

"But it's the truth."

"I know, but surely his spirit is looking out for ya?"

"Spirits aren't helpful in the physical world, and I am not about to summon him or my mom. They are resting peacefully. I won't disturb them. John, part of me wants to believe he had a damned good reason for hiding this secret, but the other half doesn't understand it at all."

"I wish I had more information to give you besides the old family cabin."

"You have nothing else?"

"No, sorry. He wouldn't tell me more. He worried about what could happen if someone extracted the information from me."

"What was running through his mind those last few weeks? I wish he would have done things differently." I said.

"Honestly, I am surprised we haven't seen your dad's spirit. I can't imagine he's truly at rest unless your mom was there to greet him."

John reached out to me, and I pulled away. This was all

too much to take in. I navigated my way down the stairs and headed back down the path to the oak tree, where I parked my bike. John followed suit. I didn't say another word the entire way. John kept his distance, but continued to follow me until I reached my bike.

I frowned and sighed. "John, I'm—"

He put up his hand to stop me. "Listen, you're upset. Parts of your life will become lies. Everything is up in the air. Where the dust settles, we don't know. I get it. You feel betrayed too. I know I do. I wish I could help further, but what I told you is all I know."

He kept his head down, shoulders still slumped. "For what it's worth, Aaima, I'm sorry. You know I'm here if you need my help."

"I'm sorry, too. Please excuse my outburst. This isn't your fault, John. It's also the first few days back at work, and it's been one hell of a ride so far. I'll stop by later. Thanks for the stew."

"Hey, before you go, I have these for you." John reached

into his coat pocket and handed me a bundle of papers. "Deeds and other things for the cabin."

"Thank you. You have my word that I won't keep you in the dark. I'll get answers for both of us." I squeezed his hand, then tucked the hefty papers inside the hidden pocket of my leather jacket.

I hugged John and hopped on my ride. I started it up and rode off. He stood there motionless, surrounded by the swirling dust. I glanced back one more time before I sped up to the highway entrance.

What a bust. First the shit with Abraxas and now this. I had the urge to party hard, but restrained myself. Confronting my problems head-on was necessary, but it seemed impossible without dad. Over the years, I had relied on him more than I realized. I was fortunate to have him. Even with all the secrets. In time, maybe this would all make sense.

I had a new clue too: the old family cabin. The trip would take several hours. It was time to head back to the DBA to pack some clothes and gear. I'd head out after a quick snooze and leave Steph to watch over the office while I searched for the truth.

CHAPTER EIGHT

SHOULD WE WORRY?

Abraxas

Aaima needed a way into the Sanguine compound. There was only one vampire who could assist her, and that was Matthias. He'd be able to secure a document with its layout. Plus, he owed me a favor for letting him hide out. He was still holed up out in Club Midnight, my father's old place.

Victor had tried to hire Assad to kill Matt–his own son. The old vamp had clearly lost his sanity. His thirst for more power was obvious, but what had he planned to further his agenda? Vampires were often corrupted by their own egos. They'd ask the same old question all of us in the Supernatural community eventually asked ourselves. Why hide? I understood the urge to be what I was and not hide it, but knew better. Assad's warning echoed in my mind: *humans outnumber the Supernaturals, they'd destroy them all.*

Not wanting anyone to see where I was going, I checked my surroundings before taking Ronan's car instead of mine. I rode through town without a trace, making sure nobody had tailed me. I slipped into the derelict building where Club Midnight once stood, pristine.

The walls were now ragged and worn from years of neglect. My hand drifted across the chipped black paint. I had spent my teenage years here working for my father. This was the place I learned how to navigate our world. Parts of me detested I had let the place rot almost to its bones.

The rustling of fabric close pulled me from my thoughts, grabbing my sole attention, and I looked up. Matt's face stared down at me from the ceiling before he released his invisible hold and leapt down to the floor to his feet like a cat.

"Just me," I said.

He studied my face as his irises flared a deep red. "What's going on? Is everything alright?"

"No, Mammon showed up. She is holding one of my amulets hostage for information, and Aaima wants details on your coven's compound."

"Ah, I knew it was only a matter of time. Aaima is a smart woman, but what is she planning? She can't take my father's coven on, alone. Shall we proceed deeper into this old ruin?"

What did he mean by that? What information wasn't he telling me? I nodded and followed him down the hallway. "Could you clarify what you meant? She wants to do a recon first. Gather intel, so she has proof before she attacks. She'll probably seek alliances in the community."

"And she needs an inside source, and that's me. How is she planning to sneak in? They'll smell her from miles away." Matt disappeared for a split second before reappearing behind the bar–his back to me the entire time. His movements were nothing but a blur.

Once he turned around, he had our favorite bourbon and two whiskey glasses already poured.

"I sent a banshee to work for her. Perhaps she plans on using him to scope it out? He could go in and get out without anyone noticing." I took the cup in my hand and sipped the amber liquid.

Matt joined me in drinking. "Smart. I am not sure I feel comfortable drawing anything out, don't want it to slip into the wrong hands, but I'm willing to discuss how the banshee can go in unnoticed."

"Are you afraid that Victor will find out if there's physical evidence of you helping?" I understood his hesitation. Victor would instantly recognize his son's handwriting and smell. Even the slightest touch of another vampire's skin on an object left a discernable scent.

"Yes. As of now, he assumes I am dead. I'd like to keep that way until my plans fall into place."

"Assad's doing, I take it? What plans?" I was curious what Matt was scheming. I hoped he was plotting to take over. It'd settle the imbalance of power Victor was gaining.

"Yes, he helped with that before I came to you to hide out. I cannot tell you everything yet. I will, when the time is right."

"Interesting. Before Assad died, he was searching for you."

"Yes, I know, but I didn't want to leave here. The trail needed to be cold or Victor would have found me."

"You know you could have claimed sanctions at the club? I never asked you why you preferred hiding out versus that alternative."

"My father needs to believe all of his coven members are with him now. My being alive would render that idea void. He needs to think he won."

I mulled over his words for a moment, taking a drink before speaking. "Fair enough. So, how do I get the layout to Aaima?"

"Bring her here. I owe her a great deal. I'll tell everything she needs to know. Her father refused to kill me, and it set in motion the most terrible events. Victor has lost all sense. There's no redemption in his future. I'll fight alongside her when it's time."

"Good to hear. May I ask...Did Victor have Assad killed for refusing to kill you?"

"I am not sure, but I suspect the answer is yes. He is heading out to greet the leader of our sister coven soon. Once he is gone, I say we go to the compound and look for evidence using this banshee friend of Aaima's."

He said 'we' I wondered if he was planning tagging along instead of hiding. "We? Does this mean you're coming with us? I thought you were afraid he'd catch your scent?"

"I'm working on a masking potion. Took some digging around in here, but I found a plethora of ingredients stashed in the lower basements. Should be ready in the next twenty-four hours." Matt was quite resourceful. I had no idea, but I had also avoided this place, because it was also my father's tomb.

"Your face tells me you're surprised. Didn't you know

about the massive stores below?"

"No, this is where he died."

"Ah. I understand now. Let's continue on. Tell Aaima I'll help in every way possible. I owe her that much, and more."

"I will. Thank you for assisting her and taking care of this matter. She deserves to know the truth. I hope the banshee finds it when we send them in.

"You're welcome. I'll see you later?" he asked.

"I'll be back as soon as I talk with her."

"Until then," Matt bowed and slipped back into the dark recesses of the club. And I made my way to the DBA.

When I got there, I quickly noticed Aaima's bike was still gone and worry flooded through me. *Where is she?* I pulled up and stepped inside the office. Loud, guttural snarling echoed from the back room.

"Fenris, it's Abraxas. Where's Aaima? I have a message to deliver to her."

"Leave, she's not here."

Another voice spoke up.

"We should hear him out." Specter said.

"Fine. He has five seconds. Spit it out devil-spawn."

Fenris and the banshee poked emerged from the back. Maybe it was a trick of the light, but I swore he'd grown since I'd last seen him. The banshee sat down at Aaima's desk and started working. She must have taken over her father's. Good, she was stepping into the role she was meant for.

"So, Specter, real name time?"

"Y-Yes. My name is Stefen."

"Thanks for that. So, update on the plans for getting into Sanguine Sanctum. I don't have a map for the compound, but I have someone who can tell us how to get in and out. His name is Matthias."

"Aaima will be happy to hear that." Stefen replied. All the while, Fenris's eyes followed me around the room. "Yes. She'll remember who Matt is too. The one case Assad didn't accept."

"She mentioned that," Stefen said.

"Do you know when she'll be back?"

"We were pretty sure she'd be back already, but she's not."

"What did she say before she left here?"

"She was going to see you and that's it."

"Should we be worried? Fenris, what are your thoughts? Do I need to call Braun?" He studied my face. His glare unsettled me. Something about him always put me on edge.

Some of it was certainly his hatred for my kind.... The rest? I had yet to find out. "Fenris, listen. I love her, I've always been neutral, stayed out of things, but for her I'd throw myself in the front lines and take the killing blow if it meant saving her life."

Fenris stayed quiet as he stalked over to sniff me. I stiffened up. He never acted this way with me before. In fact, he had chased me around the parking lot at Aaima's apartment once when we first met. I thought he was going to tear my arm off. Hells he was probably contemplating it right now.

I wasn't sure what to do, so I remained still and waited for him to make the next move. Several minutes passed before he turned to me. "You can stay until she gets back."

"You didn't answer my question, should we worry? Do we need to go looking for her?"

"Yes."

"Well, where do we begin?"

"Follow me," he said, so I did. All of three of us gathered in the break room and started going over what we needed to do next.

Chapter Nine

Back at the Office

Aaima

Frustrated, I drove back to the office at a snail's pace in an attempt to clear my head. I missed my dad, but the secrets he kept created a wall between us. I wanted to trust that he meant well, but the cost of his secrets lived with me now. Would I have enough time to find the answers I sought, or would I end up getting screwed?

When I burst through the door, I found Fenris, Stef, and Brax in the back. Bewilderment plastered on their faces. With a huff, I took a seat at my desk.

"What the hell are you guys looking at?"

Stef got up and disappeared—probably into his room. Fenris approached me first, his wet nose touched my hand. My hardened stance melted a little, but only for him. I scratched the top of his head, behind his ears, and around his neck. "Everything is a damn mess boy."

I could feel Brax's eyes on us as he shuffled over, but I fixated mine on my Direwolf and nothing else.

"Dad kept secrets from all of us. He waited until the night before his death to inform John, too."

Slowly, Brax approached my desk. "Secrets?" he asked.

I touched my head to Fenris's, staying that way for a few minutes. Brax just stood there. He was waiting for me to answer. Where did I even begin? I didn't bother mincing my words. "I'm not human, Brax."

He shook head, wrinkling his brows, and took a step back. "Not human? What do you mean?"

"What I just said. I am completely supernatural."

Brax took a few moments to absorb the information before he spoke again. "But what are you? I think I would know if you weren't human, Aaima."

"My dad said I was a race of beings that were hunted to near extinction because of our abilities."

Brax froze, fear growing in his eyes. Then he grabbed my hands and pulled me up to him. "You're in more danger than we thought?"

"I think so? I don't know." I shrugged in response.

"Who told you this? Did they tell you anything else about what you are?"

"Yes, it was John. He gave me something to go on–someplace to search for more answers. I'll take a couple of days and see what I find out."

"John? The one hunter who worked with your dad?" Brax asked.

"Yes."

Brax's eyebrow raised. "Also, are you sure the two of you need to go alone? And where is this place? At least let me send

Braun with you."

"I'm sure we can handle it, but thanks for the offer."

Brax looked down at Fenris, who was still sitting right next to me. "Fenris, I know how you feel about me, but Aaima means a lot to me. Keep her safe, please."

"Of course, she is my charge."

I froze. Fenris wasn't being ugly to him… which surprised me. I didn't expect to find them getting along. How long had Brax been at the office without me?

"Uh, what happened while I wasn't here?"

Fenris and Brax glanced at each other, then they looked at me. "I've been here since seven." Brax said.

My mouth dropped and my heart melted a little more. He'd been waiting here for hours. I darted my eyes to peek at the clock over the front door. It was nearly midnight. Time sped by when crazy things happened.

"We were thinking we needed to send out a search party if you didn't show up soon." Brax winked at me, but I could tell that they were both serious.

"Oh, is that what you guys were doing in the back all huddled together, buddy-buddy like?" I asked.

"Yes, we were trying to decide where to look and why." Brax smoothed his finger over my palm.

"What the demon said. You had us worried. Especially since you didn't return any of our calls." Fenris nuzzled my legs and leaned against me. "I'm sorry guys. Side note: it is nice to see you two getting along."

"The demon and I have come to an understanding," Fenris said firmly.

I stared at them both.

"Yes, but what sort of understanding? Brax? Fen?" I shot both a look.

"It's an understanding. We're fine. Don't worry about it." Brax shrugged.

"Fenris..."

"What he said."

"You two are impossible. Forget I asked."

"We are getting along. That should be enough, right?" Brax

smiled.

Fenris stayed curled up near my legs. "I guess so."

"Back to the question at hand that you evaded answering. What are you exactly?" Abraxas asked.

"My dad was a Sayyaad. I am one too. Well, half—my mom was a full witch."

"A Sayyaad! You need to leave town tonight!" Brax exclaimed. "You need to grab all your best weapons and just go! Get packed up while I keep watch." He went to the windows and messed with the blinds, then locked the front door of the office.

Perplexed, I grabbed him by the arm and pulled him close to me. "Why do I need to leave? What do you know?" I challenged Brax with my gaze and met his eyes without hesitation. I was unfazed by the fact that he was almost half a size taller and stronger than me. I had a fire inside me and I would use it if necessary.

"Earlier at the club, when Mammon showed up, she said she was looking for anything and everything to help her find a Sayyaad. I laughed in her face. She cannot find out about what you are. I don't trust her. You don't want to get mixed up with that demon."

"Why's that?"

"She's after power. For all we know, the vamps are in on it too. Or maybe they know what she's looking for and had that creature kill your dad? All speculation at this point."

"So many questions. First, what can you tell me about the Sayyaads? And then what about the floor plans for the vamp coven? Do you have them?"

"Sayyaads are ancient Sups with immense capabilities. I always thought they were bedtime stories to keep us in check so we didn't alert the humans of our existence."

"Hmm, okay and..." I tapped my foot impatient for the answer.

"I had to cash in a huge favor from a vampire that is no longer in their coven, but yes, I have them... in a manner of speaking."

"What do you mean by that?" I grumbled.

"He told me he'd discuss the details with us. I want to take you all to a secure location so we can figure out a solid plan."

"You gotta be kidding me! Who is this vamp? You can't expect me to send Stef in with verbal directions only. I want the place drawn up on paper ASAP."

"Relax. It's Matthias, the vamp Sanguine Sanctum wanted your dad to hunt down," Brax said.

"Really?" I stepped back and tried to give him the dirtiest look I could. He had to understand my reservations.

"Would you like to hear what I have to say first? Have some faith. When the time comes, he'll deliver the best directions straight to us. He doesn't want his handwriting to fall into the wrong hands. Victor can't know he's alive." He cocked his head to the side.

It seemed like I had little choice but to accept what Brax had to offer. I hoped it was worth it. "Yes, I'll take it. I need to figure out what they're up to, but I was going to use Stef to sneak around their compound. He's new. I can't let him take on such a big task without more to go on. How do I know

Matthias won't screw us over?"

"I love your idea. I figured it out the moment you mentioned your plan. They won't be able to sense or see him if he stays in ethereal form. Oh, you can trust Matt. I'll let you in on a secret," Brax leaned forward. "He's Victor's son."

"Holy shit! Really? My dad mentioned something about them possibly being related. He was looking for him to answer more questions."

"Yes. Matt refused to partake in his father's plans, so Victor tried to have him killed and asked your father to do it."

"Wow. Talk about serious family issues."

"Come to the club in a couple of days. I'll take you to Matt. Stefen and him can have a bit of a chat before he goes in."

"Stef, are you okay with this?" I asked.

He shook his head up and down. "Yes, I'm good with that. Verbal directions will be plenty for me, promise."

"Okay, sounds like a plan on our end, but now about you and Fenris," Brax said.

"What about us? I have the DBA to run. I can't just skip

town."

"Go somewhere new, like for a month or two."

"No."

"Stay at John's then? He's not too far away. Can't you do that at the very least? For me?"

"So look, I didn't mention it yet, but I need to go to my family's old cabin first. That trip will take a few days. And then I might consider asking John if I can stay with him, but it won't be for long. My home is here and I'm not leaving," I protested.

"Babe, I get that, but I don't trust Mammon. She's a loose cannon and she will do anything to get what she wants, and I mean anything. Add in Victor and I am scared I'll lose you. Take Braun with you for added protection." Abraxas pleaded with me with his eyes. Whoever this Mammon character was she had him scrambling to stay above water, but I needed more information on why.

"I'll head out to the cabin soon, then I'll consider stopping off at John's. Satisfied? I don't think we'll need Braun but thanks for the offer."

He took my hands in his. "Yes. Thank you," he said before planting a kiss on my cheek.

"Also, do you know if the wards are still good at this cabin of yours? How long has it been since you were there?" Brax asked.

"They should be. If not, I have my mom's spell book to take with me. I can just set up new ones, but my dad carved them into the walls of the cabin and the fence posts surrounding the property. My mom put up some too. I am sure we will be fine."

"Okay." Brax nodded, then directed his attention to Stef. "Thursday morning, come up to my office but come in ethereal form. Don't shift to corporeal until I am alone, understood?"

"U-Understood, Abraxas. Sir."

"Okay, this all sounds good. Discuss, but maybe wait till I am back?" I looked at both of them and they nodded their heads in approval.

Brax let out an enormous sigh. "I hope this goes well. If we can figure out what Sanguine Sanctum has to do with this and what Mammon is really up to, the entire community will be better off."

"Is there anything else you can tell me before we go our separate ways?" I asked.

"Nothing I can think of. Matthias is an old friend, so I am helping him hide out, and Mammon is a thorn in my damn side. She is now my equal in our community and likes to rub it in my face. I voted against her several times, so she's making it a point to put me in a bind."

"I could kill her later for you." I winked at him.

"Tempting, but I am not sure that's a good idea."

"I was joking, well, sort of." If I needed to send a demon back into the depths of Hell, I would. He only needed to say the word. I think Brax knew this.

"Let's get our intel first. I don't know if she's connected to the coven or not, but Stefen should be able to find out," Brax said.

"Well, let's do this then."

I strode over to Stef, scooping up writing supplies. My pen hovered over the notepad before I began writing. I left directions to stay in the basement and set the alarm system before leaving. He read it, then directed his attention to me. "Got it," he said, before retreating to his room.

I crossed over to the back end of the office and rummaged through my locker for some fresh clothes, putting them into my black leather backpack. Brax and Fenris waited for me by the front door.

After packing away Dad's journals and getting Mom's spell book in the bag. I opened the cabinet to get weapons–two short swords and my favorite pistol were tucked securely into a concealed carry holster beneath my jacket. I headed over to Abraxas and glanced up at his deep blue eyes. I cracked a small smile. "Wish me luck."

"May Claunth's wealth be upon you."

"Think he'll grant me it this time since I'm with you?" Brax bringing up the demon of luck had me shifting around with my senses on edge. He wasn't that worried, was he?

"I believe so. I hope the cabin provides more answers about who and what you are. I know you'll need the clarity it will bring. I, myself, am very curious."

Of course you are. You love knowing everyone's weakness, so you can use it against them when you need to." I stuck out my tongue.

"You know I would never betray your trust." Brax's face was stone cold serious.

"I hope so. But know this, break it, and I'll hunt you down myself."

"Damn, that's kinda kinky. I might enjoy being hunted if it's you." He smirked.

"Only you would get turned on by that idea." I rolled my eyes.

"I'm a bit of a masochist." He still had that stupid grin on his face.

"I'm just letting you know."

"I said I would never," Abraxas spoke the words with such

force I didn't utter more. We stood there staring at each other, waiting for the other to speak.

"I gotta get going," I finally said.

"Please be safe," he whispered in my ear.

"I'll try, but there are no guarantees."

"You know how I feel about you." Brax pulled me into him, his body against mine. He kissed me long and hard. The warmth that pooled down my legs had me melting into him.

"I know. I feel deeply for you too."

"Hard for you to say such things. I thank you for saying them to me." He nuzzled my nose and kissed my forehead.

"Goodnight, sir Fenris. I'll see you later." He bowed and then kissed me once more.

"Only a few days and I'll be back. Will you check on Stef as often as you can?" I asked.

"Of course. Also, If I call Braun, would you wait for him so he can go with? Extra protection. Please accept this time."

"No, I'll be fine." I should have known he was going to ask again.

"Okay, I relent." He smiled and flipped open his phone. "I'm going to text him quick to let him know I'm on my way back to the club though." Brax pressed the keys on his phones with his thumbs.

"Okay. Stay here for a second for me? Just to double check that all is well?"

"Anything for you," he said.

"Anything, huh?" I asked, "Better watch what you promise. I'll hold you to it."

"Counting on it." His smile widened.

"Hey Stef! I'll be back in two-ish days' time. Will call when I have a good signal," I yelled.

"Sounds good!" he bellowed from the back.

"I'll see *you* later." Brax wrapped me up in his arms.

"You're the best. See you in a few days." I planted a big kiss on Brax's lips before reaching for the knob. Brax's eyes followed us out.

We would need Dad's truck. I headed over to it and cracked the driver's side door open. Fenris hopped in. I tucked my backpack behind the front seat, slid in, and started her up. We headed back out of the city. What awaited me at the cabin was a new mystery, and I needed to get there to find out exactly what I was and what I could be.

CHAPTER TEN

THE ROAD TO FAMILY SECRETS PART ONE

Aaima

Fenris was curled up on the seat with his head in my lap while I drove. I hadn't expected to leave as soon as I got back, but it seemed like the best idea. And I had a feeling that Brax would have pushed me out the door if I hadn't agreed to go immediately.

I drove the thirty-eight miles to John's turn off but continued past on the highway for another two hours until the sun would rise.

Driving always cleared my mind. I reviewed the information we had so far, wondering what the deal was with Mammon and Brax. He hadn't divulged a ton of details. I was sure he had his reasons, but I wanted to know more.

Back in Brax's office, Braun made sure we kept quiet. Did Mammon really have eyes and ears in such unlikely places, or was merely muttering her name enough? Some demons had that kind of power, whether natural or stolen. I couldn't be sure until I found out more about her.

The what-ifs plaguing my mind stirred up anxiety. I could feel the thump of my heart pump faster in my chest, worrying about what would happen next. Just a few days back at work, and it was one mystery after another. Something had to give. Hopefully, the cabin would provide some helpful answers.

I crossed my fingers with my free hand, and Fenris licked them. He knew I was anxious. Fear settled into my body.

I had to remember what Dad always said. Fear prepared us for what was ahead. I needed to take some deep breaths and think outside myself. Objectivity was necessary. I had to release my emotions for the time being.

I knew the Sanguine Coven vamps had something against us, but what? Mammon was looking for my kind, whatever a Sayyaad really was.

The creature that killed my father took Stefen's mom. Why did they take her and kill my dad? Abraxas suggested that Mammon and the coven might be in cahoots together, but something didn't sit right with me.

If the coven controlled the beast, they either knew what he was or suspected it. So, Mammon would already know and wouldn't need Brax to help her.

Maybe the vamps held a grudge I didn't know about... something else that my dad kept from me. But the DBA was also notorious for killing vampires. We were the best in the business, and everyone knew it. But we mostly dealt with rogue or Bloodlust vamps.

We weren't just hunters. Sanguine Sanctum had paid us to take care of the unwanted vamps because it put them at risk, too. Or maybe it was the fact we denied their bounty on Matthias. What else could it be?

I felt like Mammon had to be looking for a Sayyaad for her own reasons. Victor, on the other hand–maybe it was simply retaliation for not taking Matthias down. Either way, I'd figure it out.

I needed to write everything down like Dad did. The paper trail would be invaluable in case something happened. I had the feeling that the vamps would try to take us out once they found a new weapon of choice.

We survived, and that wasn't what they wanted. Dad made it clear that the coven was instrumental in the last several cases he took. Not a coincidence.

I bet they were waiting for the opportune moment to strike? I wondered if they'd attack as a group, but if they did that, the other Sups in the community could openly attack back and I didn't think they'd risk it.

I could only speculate, but I wanted to be prepared for as many angles as possible.

Hours passed. I kept driving. I didn't stop until it was late in the morning, or maybe the afternoon. Hell, I didn't know at that point. The clock was broken in the truck, and I didn't feel like pulling out my phone to look. One thing I knew for sure was that I was tired and needed sleep.

I pulled to the side of the road. I'd sleep for a few, then move along. Not a lot of Sups liked the daytime, so I was safer to be in dreamland during daylight hours versus the night.

Fenris sat up in the seat. His head stuck out the passenger window.

"I will guard you while you sleep."

"Thank you. I love you, buddy." I tilted my head over

toward him.

"I love you too," he said, focusing on our surroundings.

I locked the truck, rolled up the windows, and kept the keys in the ignition. I opened the sunroof just enough to let fresh air in.

"You're worried despite daylight, aren't you?"

"Yes, if anything happens, you need to leave and get Abraxas. I am going to write some things down in my journal, then sleep, but just in case I need you to get it back to him and leave me to deal with whatever attacks us."

"I can't do that. What you're asking is against everything I promised. Don't make me follow that order."

"Fine, we can head to John's, just in case. But then you need to run to get more help."

"Are you sure of this?" he asked.

I recanted all the thoughts I had to him and wrote them down while talking. "Now I need to get some sleep."

"Sleep well. We'll be fine and we'll get to stay together." He nudged me.

"You get some sleep now too, even if it's for a bit. Don't worry, we won't separate. It was the worst thing to watch you get hurt, that's all. I swear I felt it. Did you feel my pain too?"

"Of course. I still do."

"Me too. I'm sorry I'm a jerk."

"No. We lost your dad. He was like a father to me, too."

"You are really so much more, aren't you?"

Fenris remained silent. We touched our foreheads together. His fur had always been soft in that spot. We stayed like that for several minutes before I adjusted my seat back so I could sleep semi-laying down. I balled up my jacket, rested my head on it, and before I knew it, I passed out.

CHAPTER ELEVEN

THE ROAD TO FAMILY SECRETS PART TWO

Aaima

I must have been completely dead to the world. I woke to Fenris growling low while he nudged me with his paws to get up. I flinched and jolted up.

"What, what is it?"

"There is something outside watching us."

I cranked the driver's seat back up and put my hands on the keys.

"Good thing the truck's locked."

"I don't think locked doors will keep this thing out."

I turned the engine on. Fenris's ear stayed erect. The fur bristled up on his back and he bared his large, white teeth.

The engine hummed while I let it warm up. It was an old diesel Dad bought for the massive fuel tank it held in its frame. My skin prickled up along my arms. I sensed the presence now. My skin always did its thing whenever my gut knew something wasn't right. I could feel the sting intensify. A single hard shiver slid up my spine.

"Fenris, can you smell it despite the exhaust in the air?"

"It's pungent. Death clings to it. I think I am smelling a... In this area and right before sunset? Impossible." He sniffed the air again and cocked his head right. "Can't be, but that's dead human flesh I'm smelling."

"Fenris."

"Wendigo! Drive. Now!"

I put the truck in drive, looked around, and pressed the pedal hard. The tires spun and the smell of rubber hit my nostrils. I felt the clunk of the truck hitting the road as it veered onto the shoulder. Paying it no mind, I continued to gun it.

That's when I saw it running up behind us. A Wendigo had found its way out of the forest and continued to race after us. I could put that thing down. What was Fenris worried about?

"Roll down the windows," Fenris said.

I pushed the button to roll down the windows just a crack.

He smelled the air again and howled.

"What's wrong now? What do you smell besides that Wendigo? I'm going to stop. We can deal with one of them," I said, despite the tingling sensation that continued to shoot through my body. But the idea of letting a Wendigo roam didn't set well with me.

"Are you sure?"

"What do you mean? Of course I am. We got this." I was surprised he was questioning me.

"There's something else out there. I can smell it, but it's not a scent I've come across before."

"What is it?"

"Don't stop. My senses are blaring. We need to get out of here!"

I let my foot do what it did best and floored it. The engine revved and the needle of the speedometer went up. I snapped a glance in the rearview mirror. The Wendigo had disappeared, but a strange darkness hung in the air behind us. Velvety black mist swirled up, billowing out and covering the road. It looked like it was midnight below the tops of the trees, but the sun was still blazing in the sky, uncovered by clouds.

"Do you see that?" I asked.

"Yes, what is it?"

"I don't know. I've never seen anything like this." I watched the darkness grow and crawl toward us. Its tendril-like arms reaching out, trying to latch on.

That had to be some kind of spell, and the reason the Wendigo was out in the daylight. But who was slinging dark magic about with a Wendigo at its beck and call? This was well beyond the norm I was used to dealing with.

"I suggest you keep driving," he said.

"You don't have to tell me twice."

I kept peeking into the rearview mirror, half expecting to see the fog still trailing us. I thought the Wendigo would jump out next to the truck, but it seemed I had outrun whoever was controlling it. A call to David and John was in order.

"Think it's safe for us to pull over?" I asked him.

"Possibly. Was that Wendigo being controlled by a witch? Things keep getting weirder the longer we're back working." Fenris was right, going back to work had opened the proverbial can of worms and there was no closing it now.

"You can say that again. I need to call David and John *asap*. They should be able to handle them—"

A loud shriek pierced the air. The truck wobbled back and forth as a large thud filled my ears. Damn thing slammed right into the truck.

"I think we need to stop or it's going to continue to attack us," Fenris urged.

He was right, so I pulled off to the side of the road and

jumped out, Fenris on my heels. I only had a pistol handy, and I didn't dare go back for my swords. We stood back-to-back. The darkness swirled around us.

I knew the fear I felt earlier meant something... that six sense was tingling for a reason.

"Get ready to fight." I scowled.

The darkness rotated around us before it built up in a circular motion in front of me. The Wendigo stepped out from the black fog engulfing it. Its long tongue protruded out of its skeletal lips, flicking the air to taste our fear.

Hot acidic fluid dripped from its sharp, curved fangs. Its skull-like head transitioned to matted fur that reached all the way down its twisted limbs, where human and monster meshed together as one. I froze. Stupid me. It glided closer and loomed over us. I felt Fenris's nose touch my neck. He had turned to help me face off our latest enemy.

Behind the Wendigo, a witch appeared. Her white hair flowed around her and hid her features. She bobbed up and down, floating in the air.

"Fuck. What do we now?" I whimpered.

With my finger on the trigger, I aimed my pistol in her direction. I wasn't stupid. I knew who had the real power here. There was no time to hesitate, either. I squeezed it and the sound of the gun going off deafened both my ears. I shook it off, but the ringing persisted.

The witch fell backward, deep into the thick mist she had summoned. Fenris leapt up and grabbed the Wendigo by the neck.

I heard the whooshing of the witch's cloak and saw the rage in her pale eyes. We were face to face. Her thin fingers reached for my throat, but a crackling noise came out of nowhere. Braun appeared right next to me and let out the most powerful surge I'd ever felt. It knocked me back and sent me to my knees. Whatever he unleashed dispersed the fog, and the witch lay crumbled on the ground. The Wendigo yowled and scooped her up, running into the trees.

Fenris started to follow them, but I called him back. Braun held out his hand and helped me up.

"Are you alright?" he asked.

"Holy... what the hell was that?" I gasped.

"Me saving your ass, but it won't hold for long. We need to get going."

My jaw unhinged. "Um, yeah, sure, but first, how'd you even get here?!"

"Abraxas texted me. I followed you."

"Of course he did. Guess I'm grateful this time. You saved us tonight."

"Sorry, he was worried. Let's head out." His eyes darted from me to the trees.

"Yes, let's!"

He jogged to the truck. The engine idled hard and diesel fumes wafted about. We all got in. Fenris laid down in the backseat with dad's old blanket. Braun sat still in the front.

I peeled out onto the road and didn't bother looking back.

***

"I don't sense them behind us," Braun said.

I eased my foot off the pedal. My mind racing. I needed to call John and David. I asked Braun to grab my phone from my pack. "Front pocket."

He handed it over, and I flipped it open and dialed our front office number. Three rings and David picked up.

"Hey, how's it going? I need you to handle something for me."

"Oh, it's going. Nice to hear from you. Was thinking you had forgotten about us over here."

"I'm sorry. I'm still struggling without him and shit's getting more complicated by the hour."

"You're all good, kid. You lost your dad. Just know I have your back."

"Thanks man, that means a lot to me."

"Now tell me about this Sup case. Is it Unsup friendly? What do you need me to do exactly?"

"This is where it gets challenging. You'll need John and every ally you can muster up for this one. If they know about the community, ask for their help."

"John is retired. Are you sure he'll be up for this?"

"Trust me, when I call and tell him what I saw, he will be."

"Okay, now you're getting me a little freaked out. I need more details."

"I was on my way out to the old family cabin for answers about my dad when a Wendigo showed up out of the blue. We barely escaped. We can't handle this on our own."

"Okay, well, that sounds easy enough. But what's the catch?"

"The catch? It wasn't alone, and it came out right before sunset."

"What the hell? Before nightfall? That's abnormal! Can you tell me what else happened?"

"There was a witch controlling the Wendigo."

There was a long pause on David's end. I knew what I was asking him wasn't an easy hunt. We only made it out of there because of Braun. Finally, he spoke. "Damn, the last time anyone fought against that duo, they didn't make it out alive.

I don't want the DBA team to end up like your cousins. May they rest in peace."

"I know. Why do you think I'm calling John in on this? He's ready, trust me. He's been preparing for a long time."

"Like I said, I have your back, but this is going to be a tough one for all of us. Are you sure you can't join us?"

"I can't. If I turn around, it's back into the flames. If we wait here, we're sitting ducks. Look, I'm sorry I gotta ask you to take this on without Fenris and me. But I'm so close to figuring out what happened to my dad and, honestly, John is who you need, not me."

"No, you're good. We got you. You and your dad saved my family. I owe you a few life debts and I plan on repaying them. If you say John is enough, he is."

"I gotta call John next. Travel on the same road you take to his place but travel further until you reach mile marker 138. Start your search there, but stop at John's first, solidify the plans, and then hunt the witch and Wendigo down."

"Got it. When will you call next?" David asked me.

"I'll be back in a day or two. I'll call on the way back."

"Sounds good. See ya."

"Later." I hung up and called John next. The moment I told him there was a witch involved, I could hear him jump into action and the iron door to the basement creak open.

"This is them. I can feel it in my bones. The same duo who killed your cousins."

"All I gotta say is, I sure hope so. I can turn around now if you think I need to. Say the word."

"No need. No one is here yet and we aren't close enough if something happens to you three. This duo has had time to build up their strength, but I've also found out how to kill them. I waited years for this moment."

"I told David to bring all the hunters he could."

"Good, we'll need the numbers. I am not sure what to expect. If it's the same pair that killed your cousins, it's the one that also attacked your parents, your uncle and aunt, and me some twenty-six years back. Almost killed all of us, but your dad got us out of there somehow. I've been gathering stories and weapons against them ever since. It better be them! It's time to put their terror to an end."

Fenris's ears perked up and I knew that meant we needed to get going.

"I need to get driving again. Fenris is sensing something. You got this for me?"

"I sure do. You stay safe, ya' hear me?"

"Of course. Fenris and Braun are here. I'll see you in a couple of days. I'll stop by your place before I head back to the DBA."

"If you want to, but if you gotta get back to business, I understand, too. Wait till you've found what you need at the cabin, okay? I'm sure we'll catch up soon. You take your time there. This can't be a coincidence. What are the chances of a witch and wendigo crossing your path?"

"I don't know, maybe? It seems the moment I stepped back into that office that everything out there started coming for me. Or maybe it's because my dad is dead. I didn't realize he had so much power, so now the craziest of Sups are coming out of the woodwork. I will take my time to find the answers. Promise you'll protect them all the best you can. Please."

"You got it. The DBA has this! We've trained and we are ready. David hasn't had a big hunt like this yet, but he needs the experience."

We said our goodbyes. I tucked my phone in my pocket and continued to drive. I hated to leave my entire team to deal with what we'd seen, but John would protect them. I knew I could count on him.

"He's right, you know. It doesn't feel like a random encounter, but like him, I don't want to read too much into things. At least not yet," Fenris said.

"That I agree with."

I spent the rest of the evening alert and speeding to get to our destination. Braun was his usual stoic self, so our conversations were light, but it was nice having the extra company. I learned a few things about him, like his favorite drink being bourbon and his love for mini golf–that was hard to imagine, but appearances could be misleading. Fenris slept most of the way. When Braun finally drifted off to sleep, I smiled.

I didn't mind the quiet that followed. I kept my eyes on the road ahead and kept driving.

Chapter Twelve

Recon

Abraxas

"If Matthias arrives prior to Aaima's return, I will call you to meet me at the club, okay?" I told Stefen as I stepped outside, the door closing behind me. "See you in a few days." that sentiment was short-lived. Matt was outside, standing by Ronan's car.

Before I could ask him how he'd gotten here without alerting other vampires, he asked, "Are your friends ready for details on my father's compound?"

I glanced back at the office door. Aaima had left minutes before. If we called and told her Matt was here, she'd turn back around. I wouldn't risk it. She needed to go to her family's cabin for answers. But Matt had taken a huge chance by leaving the old club's sanctuary sooner than expected—which meant someone had delivered a message to him about his father.

"Oh, and Abraxas."

"Yes."

"I can't go in without Aaima inviting me in."

"Oh, well, we'll go elsewhere for this then." I went to grab Stefen. Since Matt couldn't enter, I opted to head back to Club Midnight to discuss the plans.

Stefen joined me outside. His eyes widened, but he understood what was going on without words being said. He walked over to Matt and asked, "Time to go over the compound details?"

"Yes. Matthias arrived earlier than expected," I said. "We'll take Ronan's car to my dad's old club and speak there. Aaima has not invited Matt in, so it's the safest place besides the DBA. By the way, if you need to hide out away from here, for whatever reason, before she gets back, you can head to Club Midnight."

"Thanks, I appreciate your help. Ready when you are." Stef waited for my direction. I opened the car door and ushered both to get in.

I hopped into the driver's seat and Matt squeezed himself into the back, his long body stretched out across the backseat. "Well, let's hope this goes by without a hitch. I'll assume you got that potion working?" I asked.

"Yes, it was ready for a short test run, but let's get back in case the damn thing wears off."

Stefen remained silent. This banshee was eerily quiet. I barely heard him sit down in the passenger seat. Only the click of the seatbelt filled my ears. Aaima was right. He'd be perfect for the job at hand.

I put the car in reverse and backed out. My passengers barely spoke the entire way to the club. Which gave me time to reflect on the information Aaima had shared with us earlier.

Some shock remained–the woman I loved was part of an ancient race of Supernaturals and needed my protection. *Balance be damned, I'll protect her no matter the cost. If I have to choose a side, I will choose hers.*

The thought of losing Aaima tore through my being. I knew that if something ever happened to her, I'd lose all reason. Even before this, I discerned our connection when Assad introduced us for the first time. I was a club owner by night—information broker by day. They came for a dossier, but Aaima left with more–I knew she felt it too.

Despite fighting our connection in the beginning, destiny won out. I thought we made quite the pair. Demons and hunters together rarely made sense, but somehow, *we* did... a sliver of worry filled my mind. Mammon still possessed my amulet. I considered asking Aaima to help retrieve it after all. What if I couldn't protect her in my current state? I wasn't the type to dwell on what ifs, so I knew I'd have to figure it out later.

***

We crept out of the car and into Club Midnight, where the scent of a decaying building permeated the air. Matthias broke down the layout of each entrance and room for Stefen while his eyes soaked up the crude map Matt had drawn.

"My father's office will have the information you need. No one dares to enter, so his books and files will be easy to access. One of his guards is on my side. She'll have the wards removed and you can slip in unnoticed. The full moon celebrations are tomorrow. He'll fixate on the arrival of our sister coven, so it will be an easy investigation on your part." Matt pointed at the map.

"Tomorrow? But Aaima's not back. I thought we were doing this when she returns?" Stefen shakily combed his fingers through his hair. He was only a few days into his job. I understood his apprehension, but I also knew we had to do this. He was also the best man for the task.

"We shouldn't wait on this. Trust me. I wouldn't press this otherwise. If my father escalates his plans, this could be our best opportunity to gather enough evidence and persuade other Sups to support us before things get out of hand." Matt's tone was tinged with desperation.

I looked at them both. "Stefen, I understand you wanting Aaima here, but Matt's right. We should take advantage of this while we can. Let's call her and leave a message."

Stefen paused, uncertainty written on his face. "I hate to do this without her, but I'll trust you. Let's not wait."

"Also, I have several of my kind involved. Stay in ethereal form if you can," Matt added. "Abraxas and I will be out in the gardens in case something happens. If it comes down to getting you out, my people will defect and help you escape."

"I won't need to shift back to corporeal form, and I'll easily memorize all the information I gather. Unless you want to grab certain papers?"

Matt's response held no hesitation. "No, there will be time for that later. We can use an oracle to show what you saw to those who require proof."

"Also, I'm sure Aaima already told you this, but you are

capable, and I won't leave you hanging. I, we, got your back," I said.

He gave me a slight nod before asking Matt to review the map once more. When he committed the map to memory, we burned it and headed out.

Chapter Thirteen

Family Secrets Cracked Open

Aaima

After driving over three hundred miles, our destination was finally in sight. Right around four and a half hours of travel time, I knew the turn-up to the cabin was close. It was easy to miss if you weren't paying attention. Luckily, the moon illuminated the landscape ahead, making the wooden fence post with a pentacle carved at the top easier to spot.

The design was almost impossible for the human eye to

make out, but a subtle, luminous glow emanated from it. I made a sharp right the moment I saw it.

Overgrown brush engulfed the driveway, spreading from one side to the other. Low branches scraped the top of the truck, and the tires crunched over the foliage that crept along the path.

I pulled up to the gate and parked. Stuffing my phone in my pocket, I twisted to grab my backpack and weapons from the back seat and suited up. Braun followed suit, cracking his knuckles. A surge of energy emitted off him and I saw his horns appear.

While I wanted this to be a peaceful experience; I knew it was better to be prepared for anything rather than being sorry later.

I hopped out and propped the door open for Fenris to follow me in. He leaped past me, waiting for me to lock up the truck. A cobblestone pathway led past a row of large blackberry bushes and Mom's Garden. It was still in perfect condition. Solar lights lit up as we walked. It was like someone had taken the time to keep everything in shape for future use.

Braun stopped me for a second. "This is where I'll head out. I sense you'll need privacy for the next few steps."

"Thank you. I appreciate the help. But how are you getting back home?"

"Just watch what happens next." A sly smile crossed his face. "Call if you need anything. It's been nice getting to know you more."

"Same. We'll have to play mini golf sometime."

"Works for me. Be prepared to lose." He winked.

Braun twisted a ring on his right index finger. His body started dissipating into thin air. *How in the?* My jaw slacked as my mouth fell wide open, while the last part of him to vanish was his large cat-like grin.

Stunned by Braun's exit, I was at a standstill before directing my focus back to the cabin. There she was, peeking out behind two large, trimmed pine trees. Inside, the lights flickered on as if some magic sensed my approach. Our old rocking chairs sat on the covered porch and a gleaming warm light filled each window. From what I could see, everything still looked the same as it did when I was eleven.

Dad must have kept the place cleaned up. Or maybe it was the magic Mom used that had it feeling like everyone had only stepped out moments ago. Either way, it was comforting. I was home. Now, if only Mom walked out the front doors with a food tray and her famous lemonade.

I smiled at the memories, but sadness crept in around the edges. Though I looked a lot like Dad, I had many of her facial features. Like her eyes. Forest green with tiny flecks of gold, anyone not paying attention would miss them. Around the irises was a ring the same blue as lapis lazuli. She always glowed with joy and love, her warmth wrapping around everyone in the room. The pain of her absence echoed through my every thought, unable to be put into words.

Mom died a few days before my eleventh birthday. I remember tucking her dark golden blonde hair behind her ear one last time as we prepared her for a hunter's burial. Dad didn't show too much emotion, but that day he cried and cried. My throat tightened and my eyes grew teary. The intensity of Fenris's gaze burned into me.

"Memories," he asked gently.

"Yes," I whispered, voice hoarse.

We walked up to the porch. Mom decorated every step up with a large, glimmering crystal geode. There were even potted plants thriving. I paused at one in a ceramic blue mushroom and retrieved the key hidden inside, then unlocked the door. Propping it open, I let Fenris go in first. The musty air grazed my nostrils. That smell of a place sitting without life being lived in it. The source of light we saw from outside was a large lamp sitting on the entryway table.

I remembered the day we got electricity to the cabin. We

were close enough to the road that we had a line of small electric poles leading to the property. Flicking the overhead lights on, and it was like stepping into the past. Everything was exactly the way mom had it before Dad claimed he sold the cabin after her death.

The same old quilts were folded neatly over the brown leather couch. The quilts were anything but typical. They were covered in symbols I recognized, but I didn't know their true meanings.

When I was nine, I got really sick again, like I had when I was a baby. It lasted for an entire month before we came to the cabin. *The memory of my mother tucking the midnight blue quilt around me will forever be etched into my mind, down to the feel of the soft fabric against my skin. I traced each embroidery stitch with my finger over the soft golds and bright yellows until my eyes were heavy with sleep and I dozed off, exhausted from the fever. When I woke up the next morning, I was almost completely better.*

I ran my hand over the blanket. The cabin held so much

magic even after all this time sitting empty. I walked around, absorbing the scene before me. Dried herbs hung in the kitchen, homemade paper sat stacked on the kitchen table, and mom's favorite kettle still rested on the stovetop. Everything was immaculate. I cried a little. All of it was unbelievable. Like mom and Dad made sure this place was perfect for the day I returned. Fenris rubbed my legs with his head, and I crouched down beside him.

"This is amazing." I nuzzled his ear.

"Home." Fenris sighed contently.

"Yes, home."

We wandered around the living area some more, then headed to their bedroom. I figured Dad would have the answers tucked away in the closet. So I went straight for it.

At first glance, it looked like most closets do, clothes hanging, some containers and boxes lined the top shelves. Shoes sat in neat rows on the floor.

He wouldn't have made it obvious to find. I kneeled and peered into the back of the closet, the musty scent of age filling my nostrils. I pressed my hands on the walls and tried wiggling them to see if any panels moved. Nothing. I checked the sides next, holding my breath, waiting for something to reveal itself to me, but there was nothing until I checked the floorboards.

I tried several of them when a strange spark traveled up my fingers. *That was weird!* And finally, one floorboard popped up, like it had been waiting for my touch. With hands trembling, I lifted it and inside the nook was a dark wooden box with rope handles. I pulled it out and propped my back against the bed behind me, sitting on the rug lined up with the edge of the bed and closet. I had no breath left in me as I opened the lid. In the box were old leather-bound books with a note on top.

"There's a note addressed to me from Mom and Dad.

"To Aaima,

"Our sweet girl, we love you more than you'll ever know. Here are the secrets of the past. Hopefully, they'll unlock a brighter future for you. If we're not here to give this to you, just know

we both did what we could to ensure your safety. Live long, love well, and embrace who and what you are.

"-Mom & Dad

"P.S. Tell Fenris we love him too. He'll discover secrets about himself along with you."

"That's not cryptic at all," Fenris mumbled when I finished reading out loud.

"Right?" I said, "I guess I need to read these old tomes." I picked the box up and moved to the comfort of the bed itself. Fenris joining me as we settled into the many pillows propped up against the headboard.

"Why does this not surprise me? Your dad and his books."

"Records, dear Fenris, they are everything," I mocked.

"You sound just like him." Fenris bared his teeth at me. A low growl emitted from his belly as he playfully nipped at my wrist as I ran my fingers through the thick fur around his neck and scratched his sides.

"Well, here goes nothing." I cracked open the first book beneath the note.

The pages within were beautiful. Someone had written every passage by hand. Each picture painted to near perfection. Passage after passage detailed the supernatural. The left side held the text, and the right side was always a drawing. Each so detailed and beautifully colored in.

"Wow, look at this!" I flipped through a few pages with the tome turned so Fenris could see it.

"Looks like it is in alphabetical order, too," he said.

"Let's check out Direfolk... Direwolves," I murmured.

Enthralled by the contents, I stared at the pack of giant wolves standing in a golden field with a forest behind them. They were ripping the chains off the biggest wolf in the middle. He was solid black, just like Fenris, but he was the size of a mammoth.

I showed him, then read the passage out loud. "Direfolk are descendants of a godlike creature that is often associated with Norse mythology. They were giant wolves cursed by an unknown witch in centuries past. Now they are smaller and easier to control."

Fenris snarled.

“Look down here. I pointed to some notes scrawled in the margins. Dad made notes. He said that you can’t control the Direfolk like the book says, but they choose certain individuals to be bound to.”

“I chose you,” he said solemnly.

“Do you remember how you came to be with us?” I asked him.

“I remember being with my pack talking to my father. I had become restless and weary. He had me choose from six stones. He told me to touch the one I was drawn to most. I did, and I saw the flash of a small girl, you, in its reflection, and I knew. My father said to prepare myself and then he uttered a deep guttural language, and everything faded into darkness. Then I heard your cries when I came to. I was sitting in your room. You were in your crib, blankets tucked around your small body. Confusion overtook me, but my father shared one last vision, and it all made sense. I curled up next to your bed and I’ve been with you ever since.”

"I didn't know that. Why didn't you tell me sooner?"

"You didn't ask."

"Humph." I gave him an exaggerated pout.

"Let us move on. Go to S," he urged, bumping me with his snout.

"Okay, okay, no need to get pushy," I teased.

I flipped the pages and found Sayyaad, and many other names for what I was, all with similar meanings: hunter. Well, it was fitting, but I expected more. Perhaps ambiguity was the intent - leaving me grasping at hidden meanings and vague possibilities. A hunter could be anything and anyone... Vampires and demons hunted my kind to near extinction because we rivaled them in strength, and sometimes we could easily exceed it. Our abilities terrified other Sups. Certain Sayyaads gained the powers of others.

"This is interesting. It says some Sayyaads can absorb powers with a single touch. If done with focus and spell work, it doubles. Is this our strength? Think about it: we had never faced the creature before. It attacked us first before we could take on its strength. I bet the storm surrounding it also inhibited our abilities. And this is why it killed Dad."

I turned the page and kept reading. A picture of a female warrior–who looked a lot like me–with the giant black Direwolf stared up at me. Down below it, in my dad's handwriting, were our names. Aaima and Fenris. What did it mean? *Why did she look like me?* My heart pounded as I read about a prophecy of a warrior and a Dire companion, both so strong that none could stand in their way. According to this text, they'd stop a great evil in the future. Did my parents believe we were part of something far greater?

My thoughts scattered as I felt Fenris's breath on the side of my face. He may have had a wolf's body, but his mind was sharp as any human's.

"Is this us? Is this why your dad kept your origins a secret?" he asked, peering over my shoulder.

"Come on, it's just an old story." I drawled, barely believing the words myself.

"What if it isn't? What if your dad and mom figured out it

was about us?"

My pulsed raced with the possibilities, but I stifled it with a deep breath. "I don't know. This is too much."

"Why? Life is never what it seems. What if we could be more? Wouldn't you want that?"

"Yes. No. I don't know. Let's not forget the prophecies Dad shared with us and how they didn't happen as expected. I don't think we're invincible."

"Not invincible, but strong enough to win the fight. Strong enough to take out Victor." Fenris nudged the back of my arm. "Think of all the tales out there. They're mere reflections of the truth."

"You're right. Just seems too fantastical to me." I shrugged.

"But what if it means we'll be able to kill the creature that murdered your father?"

A wave of determination rippled through me and I whispered, "You make a good point. Let's keep reading."

Chapter Fourteen

Stay Awhile Longer

Aaima

I spent most of the night and all the next morning devouring each book in the box. Paying close attention to everything I could find about Fenris and me. The prophecy thing still seemed bogus, but there were some strands of truth to it I couldn't deny. My dad mapped out the connections when Fenris magically appeared in my room.

His own father told him the same tales when he was a kid himself. I wondered why he hadn't shared these stories with me. Why was I only finding out about them now? Had he planned to tell me at all, or was it because he thought he had time?

"Man, if only I was a teenager, I'd believe this shit." I laughed.

"There is truth everywhere. You just have to go looking for it." Fenris laid his head on my shoulder

"Between you, my dad, and this bullshit." I said, gesturing toward the stack of journals. "It's a lot to ask someone to believe."

He looked unamused.

"Look, I can get behind some of this information, but not all of it."

A low but playful growl emitted low in his belly.

"Let's go with the believable bits." I offered.

"Fine." He sighed.

"So, here's the deal with the power absorption. From what I understand, our energy matches the other Supernaturals most of the time. But we need to have direct contact with the other Sup... and even then, it doesn't always work out perfectly. Like unfocused absorption isn't as powerful as focusing on taking in the strength of the Sup you touch."

Fenris contemplated briefly before saying, "That would explain why the storm-covered creature hurt us. We've never faced it or touched it before. Does this mean the next time we face the beast, it will be a fair fight?"

"I sure as hell hope so, or we're screwed."

"What else did you read?"

"Well, my mom left a massive grimoire in the box. There are a ton of spells. I think the most fascinating thing is the witch that wrote it said to get certain symbols tattooed on oneself to channel the energy of spells more fluidly if the witch blood was mixed."

"Something to think about."

"I have a few tats already. What's a few more?" I shrugged. "Especially if they help with spell-casting. We both know I suck at the magical end of things."

His ears perked up as he considered the possibilities.

"Maybe you can finally get the glamor to work on me for longer?"

"That would be nice! No one would know your true size, and we could roam about more freely. Not that I think people really notice anyway, at least not in the city. Everyone there is too consumed by their own lives. But you're right, we wouldn't have to stop every five hours to recast."

"Truth. But we still need to be careful, otherwise your dad would be right—humans could end up being a danger to the Sup community. We need to protect our own, particularly the ones that deserve it."

"Agreed. What should we do next? Everything needs to stay here where it's protected. We can't risk anyone getting their hands on this information."

"Head back to the DBA? And only take what we absolutely need to? Put the rest back where we found it. There was something magical there. I felt it in my hands. They will be safe." I rummaged through the pile of books before grabbing the biggest grimoire with black leather binding.

"We can if you're ready to go."

"I want to stay a while longer. One more day?"

We stayed. I wanted to be in the cabin forever. It had my parents' love and energy in every nook and cranny. I never felt more at home than I did here. I placed the journals back where they belonged and headed outside to tend the garden.

Right before we walked out to the truck, I grabbed and folded up the quilt from the couch, tucking it under my arm. I wanted a piece of Mom with me. When I got back to the DBA, I'd be sure to grab Dad's jacket and wear it from now on too.

I closed the door. My feet were heavy and unmoving. I wanted to stay, but I knew there was work to do. I would need Abraxas's help with the tattoos when I returned to the city.

My heart ached at the thought of leaving. I had to visit the cabin more often in the future.

After we figured out what we needed to do with the vamp coven and Mammon. I had a feeling we were in for the fight of our lives. The storm-covered monster was only the beginning. There would be harder battles to be fought. I secretly prayed we had the crazy strength my dad's book claimed we possessed. Without it, we'd be dead, and we both knew it.

Chapter Fifteen

Wanted: Dead

Aaima

The ride back was uneventful, peaceful even. A little too calm if you asked me. David called me the day we left and caught me just as we got to an area with better signal. Their hunt was successful, but several of our own had gone to the hospital or Doc Quinn Shayne. We were lucky to have her at our disposal. She had fixed up Fenris and me after the creature's attack. I'd make sure to send some funds her way to keep her supplies fresh. I figured we might need her services again soon.

We kept a watchful eye on the area we saw the Wendigo on the way in. It was eerily quiet, but I could sense the magic John used around the place. It tickled up my arms, softly trailing up to my neck and then traveling down my spine, leaving a burning sensation behind. Whatever he did was super packed and juiced up.

I pulled up to the DBA late Sunday evening. I really needed to pay attention to the time better, because I'd spent more time at the cabin than I'd intended. But it was hard to leave and with everything that had happened so far. It had been the reprieve I needed.

Head hung low, I took my sweet time going in, Fenris trailing behind me. I was so absorbed in my own thoughts I didn't immediately hear Brax or Stef walking up to me until Brax scooped me up in his arms, giving me a hug. It took me by surprise, and I tackled his ass until his blue eyes flashed before me.

In one swift motion I grabbed Brax's arm, using his momentum to flip him to the ground. He landed with a heavy thud, a puff of dust rising up around him. I pinned him down, knees on either side of his chest, his wrist locked tightly in my grip. He struggled, muscles straining, but couldn't budge an inch under my hold.

"Whoa, what the—?" His eyes went wide with shock and confusion. "What's this about?" he yelled up at me, voice incredulous.

I stared down in utter remorse. "I, uh, I'm sorry. You just—" I stared deep into his eyes, my face edging closer to his.

He gave me a crooked smile. One side always curved up more than the other—and for some odd reason, I loved it.

"No apology needed sexy. I don't mind this one bit, but in the parking lot? And with an audience, no less? I'd like the use of my hands if you would, please." His eyebrows tweaked up and down; the smirk on his face grew. I tripped over my words sputtering nonsense.

"Listen ...here...you, de... I, you..."

Heat flooded my cheeks as laughter erupted around me. My mortified blush must have turned my face red based on their cackling. I tried to bite back with a witty remark, but embarrassment glued my tongue to the roof of my mouth. Fenris tipped back his head, letting out a long, teasing howl. Stefen clutched his stomach, unable to catch a breath between fits of choking laughter, and Brax just planted the biggest kiss on my cheek.

I did not realize having feelings for someone could elicit such a reaction from me. I hated being vulnerable and hid behind the party girl facade for too long, but in that moment, I was me, and I wasn't sure how to respond.

"Oh, no, I see. Did I catch the almighty Aaima off-guard?" he teased.

I playfully punched him in the gut and got up. I didn't want to admit he was right yet, but I held my hand out to help him up.

"We'll just say you were keeping me on my toes. Can't slack where there are vamps to hack."

My choice of words had them all laughing again.

Brax dusted himself off. "I'll make it a point to test out your skills whenever we meet." He smiled bigger and wider. "So, whatever you discovered... it's more complicated than we considered?"

"*Weirder* than we expected." I laughed.

"Tell us more. We got some news for you too."

"What kind of news?"

"Did you forget we sent Stefen into the middle of the vamp coven?"

"Oh shit! You guys already did the recon without me? Why didn't you call?"

"Matthias was in a hurry, so we did what needed doing." Stef said. He shrank back a bit and grimaced. "What? That doesn't explain why you didn't call?" I spat out.

"We left you a message. It's okay. I figured you found some heavy shit and needed time to process," Brax said. "Just hear us out. And look Stefen is okay."

Shit. I hadn't listened to all my voicemails, but it still got under my skin. "I see that, but still." I narrowed my eyes, glaring icy daggers at them.

"Let's head inside," Brax insisted, his voice tense.

"Yes, let's." Stef quickly nodded, glancing over his shoulder.

"There are prying eyes around." Brax scanned the surrounding woods warily. The shadows seemed to swirl with unseen energies beyond our perception. He didn't have to tell me twice. Everyone rushed into the office, making their way to the back room. I decided to experiment, so I grabbed the grimoire and picked up a piece of black chalk my mom left with it.

I went through all the doors and windows, drawing symbols of protection around each corner. Then I drew one last symbol right in the middle of the door. This one kept out other magics and didn't allow anyone to listen in.

"Damn, what spell casting is this?" Abraxas's hairs stood straight up, gooseflesh on his arms.

"Something from this grimoire my mom left me. Here, look."

"That is some powerful and ancient sorcery. Damn, your mom must have been formidable." Brax shuddered.

"Is it affecting you badly?" with a swift move from my hand I shut the book and examined him.

"Yes, and no. I can definitely feel the potency of each sigil used. But I don't have ill intentions toward you, so I am safe to stay. They hurt a little going up—demonic spawn issues and all." He winked devilishly and made a show with his horns.

I bit my lip, *damn there he goes again* my nether regions all hot and bothered. "Sorry. I had no clue. Is there something I can do to help?" I replied, shifting my weight from one foot to the other before reaching out to touch him.

"Oh, there's definitely a way you could make it up to me," Brax said, his voice dropping lower as his hand slid around my waist, fingers pressing into my hip. He leaned in close. "But we'll save that for later."

He pulled back, hand trailing across my lower back before falling away. His tone regained its serious edge. "We need to protect this place from here on out. It's too important to our community."

He gazed at me; eyes intense. "I am glad you discovered such a powerful spell to protect the DBA." The firmness in his voice sent a little shiver through me. This was a side of Brax I hadn't seen before.

I stood there for a moment, trying to take in everything he was saying. I remembered hearing stories about how my dad and Abraxas hadn't always gotten along. But I couldn't imagine what it must have been like for them to put aside their differences and work together.

Brax noticed me idling and let out a deep breath. "Your dad created this as a haven, just like my club. We both knew that to keep the Supernaturals safe, we needed neutrality," He continued. "Assad and I had our differences, but we still worked together for all the Sups in this city and in this state. I miss him. He was a good man."

His words hit me hard, and I struggled to hold back tears. "Thanks for saying that. It means a lot to me," I choked out.

Brax nodded solemnly, then straightened up and changed

the subject. "Now, back to this grimoire business. Tell us more about it. I'm curious. I've dealt with witches before, but this is something else."

"Well," I began, tentatively, "we all know I suck with magic, so I am hoping we can use it to help us out a bit."

"Sounds good to me. We need an edge after what Stefen told me."

I glanced between the two of them, wondering which one would break the bad news first. Stefen sighed, his gaze downcast and avoiding my own. Brax ran a hand through his hair, brows furrowed in worry as he looked at us.

I asked, "Stef, can you tell me what happened while I was away? What did you find out while at the Coven's compound?"

Stefen's facial expression was grim as he turned to keep his focus on me. "I don't know where to begin. There's a lot to unpack, but I do know this—they still want you dead."

Chapter Sixteen

Teach Me to Fight

Aaima

His answer didn't surprise me, but the words still sent shockwaves down my spine. Death is often unexpected and terrifying in its own right. It's a strange thing to witness death firsthand, and it leaves an indelible mark on your soul. The thought of more than a couple of vampires coming after me made my skin crawl.

I had sat on Death's doorstep and lived; I understood it more than most. I didn't like the possibility of facing a vampire hoard. And they wanted to make sure I was dead so I couldn't link them to Dad's death.

I knew Stef's information was correct. The Sanguine Coven was planning to kill me. I also understood why they were taking so long to finish what they started, knowing what I was now. To succeed, they required something that would give them an advantage over me. Unfortunately for them, I wouldn't give them the satisfaction. They wouldn't know what hit them when I was done with their undead asses.

"Of course they want me dead. They need to finish the job to cover up what they did to my dad. Anything else?"

"The creature that attacked us, it's there, locked up in magical chains. It looked miserable. They're forcing it to do their bidding."

"It almost sounds like you feel sorry for it." I paused. "And what do you mean by being forced to do their dirty work? Magical chains?" I glanced over at Brax who stayed silent. He leaned up against the wall, arms folded, and listened. Stefen continued to tell me what he had seen.

"When we arrived at the compound, a group of the vampires were fighting the beast and then a woman appeared. I'm thinking she's a witch. She cast some sort of spell, waving her hands around in this intricate pattern. The creature fell unconscious before being chained back inside this large cage."

His answer took me aback. I hadn't expected that.

"Sometimes the fiercest beasts are the biggest softies," I murmured.

Stef continued. "I honestly think there's a good chance the creature is mostly harmless since they are using magic to force it to attack."

He was right. Most Supernaturals weren't out to get everybody around them, and I knew better than anyone that looks could be quite deceiving.

"Did you get a good look at the witch? Could you draw her for us? Oh, and did you find any clues about your mom while you were there?" I fired off several questions at once before giving him a chance to answer.

"Yes, I did. Silvery hair, dark velvety purple dress," he

paused. "I didn't see my mom there, but I heard some guards talking about a banshee escaping. One vamp said, 'I'm sure Victor will pull out a fang if I screw up again.' And that was it." His face twisted up with sadness and confusion.

I tried reassuring him. "Well, that's good news. At least you know she's okay and out of the coven's grasp."

"This is true. I just wish she'd contact me. It was a couple of days ago. I don't understand... if she's not there anymore, why hasn't she looked for me?" Stef's facial expression gutted me. He looked so defeated.

"I'm gonna be honest. I think she's deliberately staying away, avoiding you on purpose. She's your mom—why risk you? I remember my dad hid me once during a hunt gone bad when I was thirteen. I was mad back then, but I get it now."

My heart broke for Stef. I wished there was more I could do to help with finding his mom, but something seemed off. The one vamp was worried more about his errors and less about her. It made me wonder. Why did they want with his mom? And maybe she wasn't their first target.

"You might be right," Stef said halfheartedly, shoulders slumped.

"Hmm, they might have wanted you instead." Brax suggested. He had a point.

"What do you mean?" Stef asked.

"Think about the ways you've helped Aaima and your ability to hide in ethereal form. They may have wanted you over your mother. I have banshees working for me, and they're not as quiet as you are. You're also male, and most banshees are female. You're a rarity. I'm thinking you have untapped abilities you're not aware of," Brax said.

"I don't think so." Stef shook his head from side to side.

"Brax just hit that nail on the head, my friend. Your mom hid you from the world for a reason."

"What is it, though? She said nothing to me." Stefen looked perplexed.

"To protect you. There are ways to get a banshee to feel pain and share all the details." Brax narrowed his eyes and turned to me.

"Better that he doesn't know... right?" I said.

"I think so. It makes sense to me. Much like your dad not telling you that you're a Sayyaad."

Fuck, Brax had a point. If I knew, would my foolish teenage ass have told the wrong person? I understood why he kept it a secret, even if I hated that he did.

"Let's review what we know. Banshees can slip into an ethereal form. They have premonitions of death, a scream that can shatter glass and subdue enemies, but what does Stefen have that other banshees don't?" I asked.

"I've actually never had to use my scream and my premonitions suck," Stef piped up. "It's pathetic, really." He lowered his head and tucked his hands up toward his chest.

I studied him for a bit. If he didn't possess the same abilities as his counterparts, what was the big deal? "Scream right now," I urged him. "Let out all your pain at once. I want to test something out."

"Are you sure? My scream differs from my mom's, and she always asked me not to do it."

"I'm sure. Go for it. Like I said, think about the loss of your mom and focus on how that makes you feel. It should help you figure out your wail."

He stood up and opened his mouth wide. A faint whistling sound escaped his lips. Brax and I looked at each other and shrugged. Nothing shattered, no ear-piercing scream to bring us to our knees, but then I glanced over at Fenris. He shook his head back and forth repeatedly before tucking it down between his front paws like he was trying to cover his ears. His long tail tucked between his legs–they began shaking.

His entire body collapsed to the floor seconds after, as he convulsed in fear. "Oh my gods! Stop! Stop!" I yelled, before shooting over to Fenris's side. "Please! Stop!" I cried. I scooped Fenris's trembling body into my arms the best I could, rocking back and forth.

Stefen's eyes expanded with terror as he rushed over to us, apologizing over and over. "I'm sorry! I didn't know! I didn't know..." His voice shook before he fell down to his knees beside us.

I hugged my wolf tighter, my stomach queasy and my head spinning. "Fenris? Talk to me," I pleaded, stroking his furry head.

Stef buried his face in his hands. "Oh my gods, I—I am so sorry."

Brax's hand met Fenris's side. Everything around us fell silent. I wasn't sure what to do next. How could we help him?

Gradually, his body stopped shaking, then he went limp in my arms. A strange heaviness overcame me and I tried to shake it off, but as I stared down at his face, his eyes bored into mine with an intensity I wasn't used to. His voice filled my mind for the first time in months. *Lay down.*

Dizziness spiraled through my skull when I tried taking a breath. The edges of my vision filled with blackness. Brax and Stef called out our names. Then everything faded into darkness.

"Your scream is so high-pitched that we couldn't hear it, but it almost did Fenris in and somehow this affected Aaima too. Her pulse and breathing have returned to normal and so has his." Brax's hand came into view as he stroked Fenris's side. "*If* they don't wake, I'll call someone to come assist us, okay?"

"No need." I breathed out. "I'm awake. How's Fenris? Boy, are you there?"

The seconds before his answer were the longest I had ever endured.

Fenris licked my arm, his eyes locked on mine. "I'm all right, but that was intense."

"Gah! Don't scare me like that." I was on the brink of tears and had to swallow my emotions. No way would I let Brax and Stef see me like that after already passing out in front of them, so I pressed my face into the soft fur of his neck for a few seconds before pulling away. I kissed his ears and stared deep into his eyes to make sure he was all right.

Brax scratched behind Fenris's ears. Even Stef reached out to pet him.

"Ah, a wolf could get used to this," Fenris said.

"Well, now we know. Stefen's banshee scream targets animals or beast-like supernaturals. But that doesn't explain why you blacked out with him," Brax said.

"Worry less about me and more about Stef. I bet that's why the vampires zeroed in on you and your mom." My eyes locked with Stef's. "I get it now. They can't control that creature, even with a witch at their beck and call. Not even magic can truly contain it."

Stef looked upset. I knew he was beating himself up over what happened, but he also did not know what he was capable of. Not once had his mom told him how to control his abilities. We'd have to make a trip back to the cabin soon. I bet that old Sup tome would have answers for him too.

"We need to keep him hidden. I'm telling you right now, Victor would be all over this place in an instant if he knew and you need to hide too."

"Yes, but where? Send him to stay with John, or maybe we all go to my family's cabin?"

Stef cut in. "I'm right here folks, this conversation is about me, and I'd like to put in my two cents, if that's okay."

"You're right, sorry, I just... you've been great, my friend. Facing each new obstacle head-on. You've stepped up despite your circumstances, but Brax and I have years of training with fighting. That creature whacks you once, and you're stuck in your corporeal form, remember?"

"I know, but there has to be something I can do to help. I don't want to go back to my old life, where my mother had me locked away. Teach me to fight, please." He begged me.

Stef had a point, but I also knew what happened when you went into a fight you weren't quite ready for.

Chapter Seventeen

Wild Card

Aaima

We needed to make some decisions, and we needed to make them fast. We went back and forth on what to do next. Brax wanted Stef and me to leave town. But I was more than willing to take the fight to Victor.

Abraxas fought against the idea of me going in and slaying as many vamps as I could. I was fully prepared to eliminate them if necessary. Even if it almost killed me. He quickly reminded me. *This is what they want.* I knew he was right.

They already took my father away from me. I couldn't give those bastards the joy of taking us down.

"Before you do anything, please let me tell Matthias. There are many who don't agree with Victor and will follow him instead. I want to give them a chance. They deserve it."

"Of course, I agree. Like my dad always said, we only hunt the ones that wreak havoc on the world and upset the balance."

"I don't want you to do anything if you have vengeance in your heart," Brax said, face twisted with concern.

"But it would be such great fuel for me," I mumbled, rolling my eyes.

"Funny to hear that coming from a demon." Fenris snorted.

"Not your average devil." Brax winked.

"I guess not, means I dislike you less than I did last time."

"There's a compliment tucked in there somewhere, wolf."

Fenris's lips curled up, his teeth bared in the best approximation to a smile that a wolf was capable of. Unsettling and perfect. I thought it was cute, but in all honesty, it was a bit terrifying for everyone else in the room.

"That's one hell of a smile." Brax chuckled.

I grinned. "Isn't it though?"

"Well, how do we execute this plan? Victor wants power. We can't let this stand. What about the Infernal Council? Wouldn't they want to stop a rogue vampire?" I knew little about the inner workings of the demons and their council in America. Brax was our only way in, and he had to convince them to help us.

"I can talk with the council. Demons can be fickle. So Matthias is our best bet. He would need at least three days to ensure his message spreads to the right people."

"How will that work?" I asked.

"Since you and your dad denied Victor's bounty, Matthias has been in hiding, pretending to be dead to avoid Victor. But secretly, he's at work gaining new followers from the coven. A lot of them think their leader has gone mad, and they'd defect once Matt gives them the signal."

"Okay, sooo... how does that help us?"

"We tell Matt what we plan to do. The vampires on the inside will help us fight. I'm sure once I tell my fellow demons what he's up to, some will join us in the battle to come."

"Even the thorn in your side?" I asked.

"Yes, even Mammon would tear that coven apart. A lot of us prefer being here versus the alternative and he's jeopardizing the Supernatural community."

"And how many supporters does she have at her side?" I needed to know.

"She has plenty, but that's inherently risky. While I do like the idea, because we'd have enough people fighting to win. I still don't trust Mammon. Her agenda is not clear to me. I haven't figured out why she wants a Sayyaad yet, and I don't want to be responsible if it tips the balance in her favor."

"I understand, but you made a good point. I can't take all those vamps on alone. If we need Mammon, I say suck it up and tell her what's going on." We had no other choice. If we wanted to protect the balance of power in this world and keep the Supernatural community safe from Victor's tyranny, this was the best plan. We needed all the allies we could muster up, even if we weren't sure we trusted them.

"Stefen, you've been quiet this whole time. What do you have to say to all of this?" Brax asked.

"I don't know. I want to help and fight, but I am not sure I'm ready. I also don't want to hurt Fenris again, but what if you both need me to subdue that beast?"

Stef was right. "I am one hundred percent sure we'll need you, but how do we take Fenris with us? In battle, I am nothing without him by my side." Pausing, I leaned up against the wall.

The silence was palpable as we all exchanged uncertain glances, unsure of our next move.

"That's the question of the hour. Maybe your grimoire has something that could assist us?" Brax suggested.

A sliver of an idea creeped in. "The old book I read at the cabin said I just needed to touch the other Supernatural to gain its power. So, if I focus on Stefen's energy, wouldn't we be immune? Fenris and me are connected somehow, like a thread that binds our souls together." I had to test something out and this was the best idea I had.

"Let's try it, and then we'll check that grimoire?" Brax touched the top of it with his fingers before glancing back at me.

"Yes. Our focus should be digging up more information to help us while securing allies to fight the vamps. But I want to test out my Sayyaad capabilities. I have awareness now. Let me use it to see what I can achieve."

"I am ready when you are," Stefen said firmly.

I directed Fenris to my side and walked over to Stef. I placed my hand on his shoulder.

When I was younger, my mom had taught me that witches focused by clearing their mind and keeping their thoughts on a target. She said that the bit of witch we had in our blood made the process similar when we used magic. I assumed I could do the same with this ability of mine.

I hoped she was right and concentrated on two things.

Assimilating and being immune to Stef's scream. I held his shoulder tight while my other hand touched Fenris–he scooted between my legs so more of his body was flush against mine.

A pinching sensation traveled through my arm, up into my shoulders and back. It shot down through my legs and ended at my feet. Jolting back, Brax caught me before I fell backwards.

"Well, did it work? Looked like it did," he said, his arms holding me up.

"I don't know. There's only one way to find out."

We turned to Stef. He wrung his hands together and gulped loudly.

"Go ahead, my friend. Don't worry. I have a feeling we will be all right." I smiled.

Stef let loose. Fenris didn't budge, and neither did I. "Seems like it took."

Stef sighed with relief and thanked the gods under his breath.

Brax furrowed his brow and shot me a stern look. "Now Abraxas just needs to ask a certain demon for help." I muttered.

"No. The council will be enough."

"I think you need to consider it. What is the worst that could happen?" I cracked open the grimoire and started scanning the pages. I could see Brax giving me the stink eye. He knew I said what I did for a reason. It was risky to enlist the help of the demons and Mammon was a wild card, but from what he said, it sounded like she was our best option to have enough people on our side.

And we needed the numbers to make this all work out.

Chapter Eighteen

False Leads

Aaima

Brax stayed remarkably silent while he looked through my dad's old books, and I studied my mom's grimoire. He had this look on his face, like he knew what I was going to say next when I finally gave him my full attention. I piped up and spoke loudly. "You need to ask her for help."

He pressed his lips into a thin line, then said, "You do not know what you're asking."

"I do. It's a risk, but she's the only other demon close by, ranked as high as you. What else would you have me do?"

"She will want something in return. Something I am not willing to give."

"She'll want you to find the Sayyaad." I said, but it wasn't a question.

"Exactly! I can't do that—I *won't* tell her what I know."

"Then don't."

His face twisted in irritation. "You don't understand." Brax huffed, slamming his fist onto the desk.

"Then explain it to me so I can!" I snapped back, equally annoyed at his tone.

He shook his head. "You don't understand. She has a way with people. All she has to do is touch somebody, and they become pliable—under her control. That's why I'm so worried about involving her in this situation. She could use that power against us if given the chance." His lips curved down, and I saw the flames of hell flickering in his eyes.

I crossed my arms and met his gaze. Then with determination in my voice, I said. "She won't have her way with me, if that's what you're worried about."

"She's a Succubus! Mammon would get her way and then some."

I stared at him for a long moment, understanding dawned on me. "That's why you're being weird. Listen–her touch won't work on me."

Brax narrowed his eyes. "How do you know that? Have you faced a succubus before?" he asked.

"Something like that." My hand closed the journal with a snap.

"You're going to force my hand, aren't you?" he asked with a resigned sigh.

Stef eyed us both, having stayed silent for the whole conversation. His face twisted with curiosity.

"Let's just talk with her once—that's all I'm asking."

"And you're sure you are immune to her powers?" He pressed.

"Yes. I can hold my own against her, promise."

"Now, who's being vague?" Brax snapped.

I released a frustrated sigh. "Look, it's not something I readily talk about. But I figured out I'm immune to certain persuasive powers."

Brax was silent for a long moment before answering. "Okay, I trust you. I know your dad put you through some grilling tests when you were younger, and I get it. You know you can trust me and tell me anything whenever you're ready." the tension leeched out of Brax, and his balled fist relaxed.

"I know. Can I tell you about this later, in private?"

"Yes, if that is what you need from me."

"Yep. So, what are you thinking? Do you want to try talking to Mammon or not? I want to act like I'm invincible, but we both know I'm not. I'll fight because I have to, but I'd prefer as much backup as possible."

Brax edged closer to me, grabbing my hand. "Give me a moment to think. I'll figure something out."

"Take your time. I know we can work out a plan in our favor." I knew we needed to keep my origins a secret. Victor found out and murdered my dad for being what he was. I wouldn't let some stranger have that kind of power over me.

"We can't afford for anyone else to find out about you or Stefen."

"Agreed." I eyed the clock and glanced at a sleepy-eyed Stef fighting to stay awake. "But for now, I think we need some rest. Plus, I need to speak with you alone."

Typical of me, I hadn't really soaked up what time it was again, and we all needed our rest. Both turned to me and nodded in agreement.

"That sounds good to me," Stef said through a yawn.

"Thanks for everything, again. You really are a great assistant and best friend." I said.

"You're welcome. I'll keep reading this stack come morning time." He smiled wearily, patted the large journals on the table, and got up.

I watched him shuffle into the little room in the back, leaving Brax, Fenris, and me. Fenris didn't utter a word, licked my hand, and went to the front of the office to curl up on his bed. He wanted to rest, too.

"Well, I guess we'll have that talk in the morning?" Brax whispered, before heading for the door.

I felt the need to explain. "Stef looked tired, and I figured we can sort this out later, but... what if I don't want you to go? We can still talk here and now." I asked, grabbing his arms and pulling him close.

"Where?" he asked.

"The basement area has a full-size bed." I grinned.

"Oh? It does?" he said slyly.

I took his hand into mine and opened the closet and its false backing to reveal stairs leading down. Brax followed me down, uttering "Wow!" when we reached the bottom.

"Right? It's impressive," I said, looking at the old bookcases and weapons donning the walls. There were a few old paintings of different Sups too. A black unicorn with a man that looked like my father. I figured it was an ancient family member, but knowing what I did now, it was probably my great-grandfather.

"This is amazing! Your dad was a real man of mystery. This has been under the DBA this whole time?"

"Yep."

"Hey," he started somewhat uncertainly. "I need to apologize. Mammon and I have a past."

My steps hesitated for half a second and I wondered if he noticed. "What sort of past? Were you two..." I trailed off, raising an eyebrow.

"Oh, hell no! But she sure likes to take things that aren't hers."

"When you say take, what do you mean?"

"She took something from me."

"What did she take?"

"One of my amulets," he said, lowering into one of the worn leather chairs tucked into a corner.

I leaned my back on the beam in the center of the room. "Damn, and she still has it?"

"Yes."

This was serious. Demons had objects that enhanced or

contained their powers. The fact that Mammon had been sly enough to steal one of Brax's both impressed and terrified me. Who, exactly, was this succubus, and what was she planning?

"Well, how do we get it back?" I asked.

"Ripping it off her neck?" He laughed sardonically.

"I can arrange that. Just let me handle it." I was more than willing to take a demon out. It had been a few years since I last expelled one and sent it back to hell. I needed the practice.

"I don't want to put you in further danger."

"Let me take this risk. She doesn't know me."

"I don't like this idea. She'll try to claim I'm taking sides."

"But she took one of your amulets. Isn't that against demon law?"

"Yes, and no. The council may say it's my own damn fault, and they're always inclined to go against me since I stay neutral."

"I get it now. Let me handle this."

"But, what if—"

I cut him off. "Listen, I am stronger than you think. She's

one demon whose powers won't work on me."

"It's my feelings that make me worry for you" He gazed into my eyes, and I could see how worried he truly was.

I had never seen him like this before. It felt strange and wonderful at the same time. I strode over to him, pulled him close and kissed his forehead. He grabbed my face and cradled it while kissing my lips. I savored the feeling for a moment, our noses still touching.

"My feelings for you are strong too, but don't let it cloud what we need to do next and stop with the worry it won't help. You can't predict the future, anyway. It's important that we stay in the present and focus on what we can do."

"I see your point. I should reach out to the closest, same-ranked demon. I just hate that it is her."

"So, how do we get your amulet back?"

"At a price, and she wanted a Sayyaad or leads to finding one."

"You don't think she'll budge? Would she accept something else as a trade?"

"Not a chance."

"Are you sure?"

"Positive."

"Then let's give her what she wants. You can't let her hold your own power against you and you know it."

He pulled away, shock written all over his face. "No, absolutely not! Worst fucking idea to come out of your mouth yet."

"But your amulet, I get it now. I understand why you haven't done a damn thing against her, because you can't."

"Not without causing harm to myself."

"Then let me get it back." I pleaded.

"The bitch has it in her pocket. Mocking me every chance she gets. You'd have to meet her in person, and then what? If we need her help, we can't rip it off her and run away."

"Call her right now and give her what she wants," I demanded.

"No, I can't. I can't do that to you."

"You're misunderstanding me. Tell her that the Sanguine

Coven has information on the Sayyaad creature she is looking for. It's not a total lie."

"But then the trail leads back to you!"

"Does it? Do we know if they have solid proof?"

"I don't know."

"Would Matthias know?"

"It's a possibility."

"You need to call him and figure it out. If Matthias knows this information and where it might be, we can tell Mammon, but we need to get to it first."

"How?" he asked.

"Stefen," I replied.

Chapter Nineteen

Interlude

Aaima

Brax stood up from the chair and paced the room. His silence drove me crazy. I needed an answer to my suggestion. It was the only plan I thought had any chance of working. We needed to pretend to give Mammon what she wanted and make sure we grabbed the information from Victor's office before she did.

The whole idea was madness, a fool's errand at best. But what could we do? We had to play the bait and switch to win the game. Brax finally stopped and looked at me. I stared back. He edged closer and wrapped his arms around me, kissing my neck and cheek.

He whispered into my ear, “This is the craziest idea you’ve had yet, but I think like it.”

“So, we’ll do it?”

“Yes.”

One of his hands slid down to my lower abs. I grabbed his wrist to stop him from going further.

“Before we continue, I told you I’d tell you in private. I dated a succubus in high school and through my first year of college. We figured out pretty quickly that she couldn’t seduce me with her powers alone.” I waited for Brax's reaction, but instead he listened carefully to every word I spoke. “Anyway, we were serious. I was ready to tell her who I was, as I was going by an alias to protect myself and my dad. But then she hurt me in ways I’d rather not go into further and turned against me right before I revealed the truth to her.”

The words were like chunks of stones weighing down on

my chest. My first teenage love and biggest lie all wrapped into one. The pain still lingered after all those years.

"You've never told me this before." His voice was laced with tenderness and concern.

"It hurt too much, and... well," My throat tightened and tears welled in my eyes. "Because I love you... and I'm terrified I'll end up hurting you or that you will hurt me."

Brax's gaze pierced through me as he seemed to understand the intensity of my feelings towards him, and it sent a chill up my spine. He moved closer and whispered in my ear, "I love you too. I loved you the moment I saw you and ever since." He caressed the bare skin above the collar of my shirt, sending shivers all over.

"Why? What about my past?" I asked him.

"I don't care about what happened in the past. I care about now and where we stand. You made it crystal clear how you feel and that's enough."

He quickly picked me up and sat me gently on the bed on the opposite side of the basement.

"Is this the right time for—"

"Is there ever a right time?" He kissed my stomach.

"I just—"

He pulled away. "Do you want me to stop? Cause I will."

Gah! This demon was driving me nuts. It wasn't like we hadn't done the deed. Hell, we had some crazy nights in the beginning. But this? This was different. We had said the big 'L' word to each other. The seriousness of our relationship sunk in. This wasn't sex—this was more.

"No, I don't want you to stop, but this would be our first time—"

"Sober and together," he completed my sentence.

"Yes."

I latched my fingers into his belt loops and pulled him closer to me.

He leaned over and kissed my lips, then gently laid my head down on the pillow and propped himself over me.

I liked this. I had forgotten what it was like to let someone close like this, and I wanted more.

We stared into each other's eyes for what seemed like forever. His body pressed against mine while I wrapped my legs around his waist. One of his hands took mine and held it firm before his lips crashed into mine again.I could feel his heart pounding in his chest pressed against my own. The spicy, masculine scent of his skin mingled with mine. I tugged at his t-shirt, fumbling in my impatience.

I needed more - more of his heated touch, more feverish kisses trailing over my body, more of him filling me utterly.

"Let's take it slow and savor the moments." Brax removed his shirt, then kissed his way down my neck.

Each press of his mouth sent small bursts of warmth throughout my body. He continued down my neck to my chest. His hands gliding up my shirt, and he removed it, tickling my skin as he went. The touch of his lips on my torso traveled upward, his mouth taking in one nipple, his fingers on the other.

"I want you," I whispered, my voice throaty with desire. Brax gave a low groan in response that vibrated through me.

He knew exactly what I loved. His hips connected with mine. It felt like electricity taking over me and I let out a soft moan of pleasure with every movement of his. His tongue left a trail of fire across my stomach while he unsnapped the button of my jeans. He slid them down along with my underwear, getting rid of all barriers between us.

I followed his lead and helped him take off his clothes. His right hand slid down and his fingers caressed my clit before one dipped inside.

I opened my eyes for a second to look up, and he peeked down at me before kissing my lips again. The circling of his fingers pushed me right to the brink, small moans escaping as he slid two inside me now, pulsing in and out. A teasing prelude which left me begging for more while the world around me spun out of control.

"I love how ready you are," he whispered, as his cock entered me. I arched back, lost in the sensations of motion as every inch of him filled me with pleasure. My nails raked down his muscular back. I hadn't realized how much need had built up until he touched me just so, sending waves of pleasure cascading through every part of my body.

He started off slow, his rhythm increasing with each thrust,making me moan with unbridled pleasure. My legs wrapped around the strong muscles of his back. Our hands locked in an intimate embrace, our fingertips pressing deeper into the bed with each thrust.

With each calculated and precise movement, he plunged deeper into me.My legs quivered around him as he moved faster and faster. Wave after wave of sensation rushed through me as we reached peak together.

We lingered there afterward, his heart thudding against my chest, still joined. As our breathing slowed, I closed my eyes, basking in the warmth coursing through every fiber of my being. We held each other as we drifted into blissful sleep.

A piercing howl filled the air sending us both springing into action. We grabbed our clothes and dressed as quickly as possible, then raced up the stairs to find Fenris near the front door. Low growls permeated the air, and the hair on his back bristled. I rushed to the back and grabbed a shotgun, loaded in two bullets, stuffed more in my pockets, and cocked it. Brax stood by the door, his demonic energies pooling around him.

I pointed my weapon at it. He nodded, and Fenris moved to the side.

"Ready?" Brax asked.

"I'm all set," I said.

He swung the door wide open. Peering into the night, I saw Matthias standing there, covered in blood. I lowered my gun.Matthias raised his arm, blood dripping from his fingers.

"Hey, long time no see. Now, keep that thing at the ready," he directed.

"What's happening?" Brax asked him.

"We might have a problem." Matthias pursed his lips.

Right as he did this, a breeze pushed through the door, hitting me before I saw it–a Bloodlust vamp lunged forward and tackled Mathias. They wrestled on the ground while we raced out. Brax grabbed the vamp's hair and pulled it up off of Matt.

"Take the shot!" he yelled.

I pointed the barrel at the vamp's head and pulled the trigger. The shotgun cocked back into my shoulder and I felt wetness hit me. Blood sprayed everywhere. I stepped back while Brax helped get his friend up.

"Matt, what the hell is going on here?" Brax demanded.

"Victor—he turned more of our coven mates into that and sent them to attack Aaima."

Shock enveloped me. The coven leader was purposely turning his coven mates into Bloodlust vampires. "What did you just say?" I spat out, perplexed.

"You heard me right."

"This is worse than I thought."

"I let Assad know what was going on the night before he

died." Matt frowned. "It's my fault. I gave him that lead. Please forgive me. I thought I could stop Victor and your dad thought he could too, but my father won't stop till the entire world burns."

What the hell did I just hear?

Matthias and my dad were working together in secret. A knot formed in my throat and I turned, my world spinning.

Abraxas touched my shoulder, but I ignored him and I swung around to face Matt. "Explain everything to us, *now.*" I grabbed him by the shirt.

Fenris stepped up next to me and bared his teeth.

"After Victor put the hit out on me, Assad denied the bounty he offered. Said he wouldn't get mixed up in vampire politics. Assad trailed behind me and pinned me down; asked me why Victor wanted me dead. I told him he was planning something terrible. That I knew they were after something more. Then I gave him that lead to head into the deep part of the forest east of here. Little did I know it harbored that creature, and you all went in unprepared."

Matt hung his head before glancing at me. The sorrow and pain in his eyes tugged at my heart. He knew my father, probably quite well from the way he made it sound.

I released my grip on Matt and he stood up, keeping his head down. Blood soaked almost every inch of his clothing. He gulped and took a small vial out of his pocket and chugged it, mumbling, "Just in case."

"What was in that vial?" I asked.

"An antiviral serum I created to treat Bloodlust."

"Fascinating.... So, Bloodlust is a viral infection vampires can catch?"

"Yes, a very unsightly one, too. It destroys the red blood cells in a vampire's body, making the cravings and feedings frenzied and that won't be the last of them, I'm afraid. We need to stand at the ready." He pointed out into the darkness covering the sky.

"Never a dull moment at the DBA," I grumbled. Motioning for Fenris to come to me, I glamored him quick. If any human saw something, at least we could say we were fighting off strung out crack heads.

"Be ready!" Matt called.

I stood next to him and touched his shoulder. He was an older vamp, so I focused like I had with Stef earlier, waiting to feel something, anything. Something surged through me, and I was ready to face what came next.

I looked back toward the office and glimpsed Stef slip into his ethereal form. I nodded, and he smiled before stepping back inside. Brax went back in, probably for a weapon.

Then an odd silence trickled through the air.

"How many do you think he sent?"

"I don't know, to be honest." Matt replied.

"Before we do this, do I need to invite you in again? If we need to head back inside for more weapons?"

"Yes, you took ownership of the DBA when your dad died, so I can't come in."

"Okay. Matthias, I invite you into my space."

"Thank you for trusting me," he said right before screeches broke the surrounding silence.

Brax came rushing out of the office with one of our longswords in hand. His horns were visible and his eyes burning bright red.

Four Bloodlust vamps rushed into the parking lot. Fenris readied himself for their attack. I touched his fur and felt the surge of energy between us. We were ready to fight.

Chapter Twenty

Bloody Mess

Aaima

The first of the vamps went straight for Matt, then one hurtled toward Brax. The other two stayed close to each other and stalked over to Fenris and me.

"Ready boy?"

"Absolutely. Ready to tear these pests to bits?"

Fenris lunged for the vamp on the right. He sunk his teeth into its neck and shook its entire body around like a toy before he tossed it aside and ripped the left arm from its socket. It wouldn't take him long to finish the Bloodlust vamp off.

"That's my wolf." I grinned.

The last vamp screeched loud and emitted a strange guttural sound from its diaphragm before edging closer to me. It gargled, and blood dripped from the corner of its mouth.

When severe bloodlust set in, vampires no longer looked human, their skin turned completely white, waxy looking, but translucent. All the veins darkened and were purple in appearance. They spread like wildfire on their skin. Hair loss was immediate. Some loose, scraggly strands clung to its scalp. I could make out a more feminine shape to the body, but the limbs twisted like the bones of each joint had broken from finger to shoulder. What little clothes it had left were mere scraps. The jaw unhinged itself and stretched down to the collarbone. Its fangs dripped with a dark green substance.

"Don't let it bite you!" Matt called out.

It flew forward, and I dodged its attack, veering off to the right. I needed a sword, not a shotgun.

"Stef! Sword please! In the back!"

It charged, and I ran toward my truck. I plunged my feet into the ground and flipped myself up into the bed of the truck. I could see two more vamps in the tree line watching and waiting.

"Scratch that! *Two swords*!" I bellowed, before jumping out on the other side and rushing into the office.

I whistled, and Fenris barreled toward me, falling in line behind me. He zipped inside.

Stef rushed to my side, two swords in each hand. I put the gun down on the desk.

"If you need me," he said.

"I'll yell the word scream."

"What? Will that even work?"

"I'm testing out a theory. Try here in a second when I head back out."

With the swords in my hands, I ventured out the door and was taken aback by the sudden increase in the number of vampires in the trees. There had to be ten more out there, ready and waiting. I had to eliminate the one closest to me if

I wanted a fighting chance against the rest.

I rushed into the vamp that followed me to the office door's edge. Its eyes followed mine before it made its way toward me. Everything slowed down, and I shoved the sword through its neck when it came rushing toward the door. It never knew what hit it. Its head flipped through the air before landing on the asphalt. The others screamed, and I knew it'd be a matter of seconds before they all attacked.

There was no way I was going to leave Brax and Matt to fight them alone. Stef touched my arm. I turned to him and met his gaze.

"We can't take on all of them." He lowered his head.

"Stef, I know we've only known each other a few short days, but we became fast friends, best friends, and I don't say that lightly—you can do this! If I have to stand here with vamps tearing at my sides while you scream, I'll do it!"

"Anima... no. You can't."

"But I will to protect all of you. I will keep fighting and you can too. You heard Matt—they become like animals. We need to at least try."

"Gosh, I hope you're right."

"Me too. I was hoping we wouldn't be in any fights before we took on the compound, but here we are. Gotta do what we need to make it out and continue on."

I rushed toward the tree line with Fenris by my side. Stef's mouth gaped open and several Bloodlust vamps twisted to the ground, holding their wretched hands to their ears.

The minutes and hours blended together as we lost ourselves in the heat of battle. Time ceased to have meaning; there was only the next target, the next swing of my blade. I lost count of how many vampires we cut down in that frenzied haze, but it must have been at least six more before we finally had a moment to pause and catch our breath. Panting, I scanned the area. My eyes landed on Matt and Brax, fighting side-by-side. The pair moved seamlessly, instinctively guarding each other's back as they took down vampire after vampire in a deadly dance.

I watched in admiration for a moment as they whirled

through the latest enemies, blades slashing in perfect synchronicity. The last gurgle bubbled up from their kill.

Then all was silent. No more screams, no more Bloodlust vamps appeared. We all stood there and waited. I didn't trust the silence.

Brax and Matt quietly made their way over to us. It was an easy feat for Matt, but Brax tried to keep pace and I could hear each of his large footsteps hitting the ground. He grimaced and slowed down. We all kept looking around, waiting for another attack.

We heard shrieks in the distance. There were more after all.

Victor chose to sacrifice his own people in order to take me down.

Isn't this excessive? All because I am a Sayyaad, I thought. I glanced around. "This is the final push. I can feel it. We need to head back to the parking lot and roman up. Back-to-back with each other. Weapons at readied."

"Got it." Brax breathed.

Matt nodded. "Ready."

The screeches got louder as we made our way through the copse of trees between the DBA and us.

Time was a funny thing in those seconds. We raced back to more solid open ground.

Our feet had just hit the pavement when we heard clamoring of metal and voices shouting.

“Who’s in the woods with those things?” I asked.

“I don’t know. Should we gear up to meet friend or foe?” Brax turned to face me.

“What’s going on now?” Stef shouted from the DBA’s door.

“No clue,” I said, “but I bet we’re about to find out.”

Chapter Twenty-One

Leverage

Aaima

Everyone waited for what happened next. The screeches from the vamps died down, but the sounds of multiple feet walking nearer remained. I could barely make out the shape of people emerging from the trees. The closer they got, the more I could see the details.

Braun was in the lead. He bull-rushed right into Brax and then pulled me over with his enormous arms. He looked us dead in the eyes. "I am so glad you're both alive."

"Braun, how in the—? How'd you know to come looking for me and bring this much backup?" Brax asked, perplexed.

"I might have had someone give me a heads up," Braun said, pointing at Matt. I had no words. Braun glanced down. "You look a little shocked. Are you alright?"

Brax said, "I'm not in shock, what are—"

Braun put his hand up, and Brax stopped speaking. He looked at me, then at his second in command.

"Aaima, I mean you. Say *something*."

"You're like the Cheshire cat randomly appearing when we need you, and I have no other words."

"Eh, I don't need any. Just keep that boss of mine out of trouble." Braun winked.

I chortled, then calmed myself enough to answer him. "Not sure I can make that promise."

"Also—" he paused, "—I had to call someone else."

"You didn't." Brax huffed.

"I had no other options. It was the right choice to make."

"You and Aaima are two fucking peas in a pod—Damn that

bitch Mammon!"

A soft, light voice giggled behind the trees. A figure dressed entirely in white emerged from the woods, followed by several more demons. Her eyes glowed blue and her long blonde hair swayed around her.

"Damned I am, Abraxas, but it sure looks like you needed me to help you."

I peeked around Braun's shoulders to see clearer and couldn't believe my eyes. Mammon moved over and stood next to Brax, and stared right at me. Then, her mouth dropped and her eyes blinked, and she did a double take.

I did one too.

It couldn't be... *could it?*

"Maya?" she asked.

"Amanda?"

She rushed over to me, wrapping me in an embrace. Her chest pressed against mine. The old feelings flooded in. I had never healed from that first love and there she was, standing right before me. I had no idea that Amanda, my old girlfriend, was the one and only Mammon.

She leaned back enough to look me in the eye, and then her lips touched mine. She kissed me hard and long. I pulled away.

"Whoa, hey now, calm down. You're the Mammon that Brax has been talking about?"

"And you're not just anyone either, are you, Aaima?" She licked her lips and ran her finger down to the middle of her chest before she slid her hands over my breasts. I shoved her away, but she came for me again. She roped her fingers into my pants loops and pulled me close to her.

I pushed harder and stepped back. *Fucking succubus.* I had no idea Amanda and Mammon were the same person. I knew she was a demon, and we found out she couldn't affect me and make me have sexual feelings for her. It was the reason we dated, because she couldn't elicit anything from me physically with her touch. My feelings, however... that was a different story.

"Gods, I missed you. That taste, your essence, everything," she purred.

Brax's shoulders tensed as he looked from me to her, his eyes flashing red with barely contained rage. "You've got to be fucking kidding me," he growled through clenched teeth.

"Oh, silly little boy. This is the girl who caught your eye? I get it now. Trust me, I do," she said with a patronizing laugh.

Brax's hands curled into tight fists; his knuckles white. "Fucking succubus scum," he spat.

Mammon smirked, clearly enjoying Brax's reaction. "Oh, darling! Feeling a little jealous, are you? Is it because I had her first?" she taunted, "No worries, what we had is now in the past."

Brax's fingers held onto to my shoulders as he searched my eyes intently. "Are you sure you didn't know she was Mammon?" he demanded.

I shook my head, holding his piercing gaze. "I had no idea, I swear it. She told me her name was Amanda, and I went by Maya like I said. Remember, I was using an alias back then since my dad had enemies in that city."

I took a breath, trying to defuse the situation. "Chill out and let's talk this through, okay?"

Brax studied me a moment more, then released me with a curt nod, his jaw flexing. I could tell he was still battling anger and jealousy. *What a freaking kink in events.*

"I need to chill? How? What about that kiss she gave you and the way she fondled you? Took you long enough to push her off." He fumed.

Braun and Matt stepped in.

"Abraxas, she's in as much shock as you are, my friend. Look at her face," Matt pointed out.

"Pause and use your damn brain for a second." Braun added.

Brax looked as if he might explode. This complicated things. My ex and my lover were moments from battling it out over bullshit from the past.

Brax glared down at Mammon. She looked up and smirked.

"Stand down. You can't do shit—I have one of your

amulets, remember?"

"About that. You need to give it back *asap*," I interjected.

She raised an eyebrow. "Give it back for what reason? He owes me information. Until then, this baby is all mine." She pulled the amulet out of her pocket and swung it around before tucking it back in.

I blurted out, "We know how to find a Sayyaad."

Chapter Twenty-Two

New Information

Aaima

Mammon slinked over to my side. "Say that again? Did I hear you correctly?"

"We know where to find the Sayyaad creature you're looking for." I looked down at her, then moved away.

Mammon glared at Brax before shifting her eyes back to me. "How did you find this information out?" There was a clear hint of suspicion in her voice.

"Now that the cat is out of the bag, I'll fill you in on the details. My dad was Assad and the owner of the DBA. Brax hired me because finding and hunting things are my specialty." I gave her a pointed look at her slightly bewildered expression. "Or did that not quite sink in, blondie?"

Mammon laughed, despite herself. "Point taken. You always this snarky with people who save your life?"

"Only if they deserve it." I shrugged, a small smile playing at the corner of my mouth. "We also had the situation under control."

"Sure, you did." Her eyebrow ticked up.

"If you think those vamps could have taken us out, why have Brax search for this Sayyad in the first place?"

"Fair enough. So, what did you find for me?" Mammon slid her hand up my forearm. I could sense her succubus powers entering my skin. What game was she playing at? She knew I was immune, but that didn't stop her from trying. She took a cautious step forward, trying to get closer.

I shifted my body closer to Brax and took his hand in mine. Her lips quivered, and she tried getting to me one more time, but Fenris bolted between us. He must have sensed something, or he wouldn't have interfered. She stopped, taking a step back. "Ah, I see that someone's little pet is feeling overprotective," she teased.

"I don't recommend getting further on his bad side. I'll let him tear you to shreds."

Fenris growled and bared his teeth. I decided to un-glamor him. His size overwhelmed her tiny frame, and for once, she actually looked afraid.

Good, I am tired of being fucked with.

"Listen, do you want the information or not?" I bit out.

"Yes, give it to me," she pleaded, her hands clasped together in front of her.

That shocked me. She was desperate for whatever we would be willing to give her. "Hand me Abraxas's amulet first, then I'll share all the details."

"Not a chance. You must think I'm stupid."

"Well, Mammon, my track record of honest dealings is better than yours," I said.

She knew I was right. Besides hiding who I was, Mammon knew I didn't lie about anything else. She understood why I did it. Why I used an alias. It was the one lie everyone the Sup community let slide. Because it meant we got to live another day or, for the lucky ones, the rest of our lives.

"Fine, but I will only hand it to you—and alone, in your office."

Brax grabbed me and looked into my eyes. "I don't trust her, don't agree to do this."

"It will be fine. You know I have the information. It's the perfect exchange."

He fought me a bit more before giving in. Mammon and I walked inside the DBA while Stef slid into his ethereal form. The bitch was none-the-wiser.

The door was barely closed when she tried to push me to the couch. Telling me she always loved me, still wanted me, and regretted the night she broke both our hearts. Her irises had a faint blue glow.

I knew she would do whatever it took to ensnare me, but

why? Had she forgot I was immune?

I sighed, “You had a choice to make, and you made the wrong one. It’s too late now.” Brushing her advances off.

“Why does it have to be too late? Brax is weak. In the end, he’ll stay neutral and won’t help you.”

“No, Brax understands the balance needed for our worlds to coexist. His choices keep that balance. I stand with him.”

“Ugh, that stupid demon and his neutrality. I can’t imagine why you think he’s the one for you.” She asked, stroking my arms and trying to play with my hair. I pushed her away with more force this time, my frustration boiling over.

“Stop touching me.”

“Do you even know what he’s done?”

“Oh, my gods, you’re trying to turn me against him. You don’t think I know everything? If you think he’d hide things from me, then you’re mistaken. There’s one thing that he has that you don’t—*loyalty*.”

She finally took a seat and kept her hands to herself.

“Give me the amulet. Now.” I held my palm out.

"Fine." She pouted.

Mammon took it out of her pocket and shoved it into my hands. The amulet was shaped like a crescent moon. Woven intricate spirals of wires and black jewels cascaded around the talisman. Studying it closer, I noticed a clasp holding it shut. It was also a locket. I wondered what was inside and if I could pry it open. But decided I'd wait until I finished dealing with Mammon. She stormed back to the couch and plopped right down.

"Mad we're not going to fuck?" I laughed.

"A little. I'm used to everyone giving in and I forgot my touch doesn't work on you. But I saw your face when you realized it was me—you still have feelings for me, I can sense it."

"Wrong. I'm still holding on to hurt. I don't have those types of feelings for you anymore."

"Interesting you'd admit that to me."

"What? Are you planning to use it against me? Do it! Give me a reason to show you what I'm really made of." I balled my fists up. She hadn't changed. Hell, if anything, she had gotten worse.

"No, I wouldn't. I might manipulate others, but I won't start something I cannot finish." She dusted her hands off on her pants and folded her arms over her stomach.

"Good, let's get on with this." I hung Brax's amulet around my neck.

"Don't do that! Get that off your neck!" she screamed, scrambling off the seat of the couch.

"I don't trust you. Where else should I put it?"

"You're not a demon, you're just a hunter. It could hurt you!" She zipped to my side, reaching for my arms. She had genuine concern, and I was confused.

"I have more Sup in my blood than most. I am fine."

She looked puzzled when nothing happened to me as I placed it around my neck. Her eyes scanned me up and down. "How?"

"Might it be that the amulet knows where my loyalty stands?"

Stef covered his mouth with his hands. He didn't want to give himself away, but I wasn't holding back for Mammon. She didn't deserve my kindness.

"The amulet is in your hands. Now, tell me about this Sayyaad."

"Sanguine Sanctum has the information." I crossed my legs and leaned back onto my desk.

"How do you know?" she asked.

"Did you not see Matt out there? He was part of that coven before seeking asylum at Brax's club."

"Oh, I didn't realize. Tell me more," she cooed.

"Victor has it in his office, according to inside sources loyal to Matt."

She scrunched her brows. "So, what should I do? If I try to get the information from them right now, it may start a war."

"It's already begun. Victor is purposely infecting his own coven with Bloodlust. He even had a cure created by Matt, but is amassing an army of them, anyway. Those vamps we dealt with are only the beginning. Victor thinks my dad hid the Sayyaad you're looking for and killed him for it. Now he's after me for poking my nose around where he thinks it doesn't belong."

"Well, do you know if your dad hid a Sayyaad?"

"He said nothing to me about it. Those vamps have tried to kill me twice because I went looking for answers."

"I'm truly sorry for your loss. This information changes everything. The Infernal Council can't turn a blind eye this time."

"I hope you're right. Can you tell me more about them?"

"I am sure Brax has filled you in. They are the highest level of demons. They ensure we can live comfortably between Hell and this world if we so choose." She played with her golden locks, twisting them between her fingertips.

"And that's it?" I asked.

"Pretty much. Demon politics are... complicated."

"Well, will they join the battle at hand?"

"For this? Yes. What now, Aaima, the almighty bounty hunter?"

"Not almighty, but you have your information — Brax has his amulet back, and now I can get back to business."

Mammon watched me with a careful eye. I knew she was trying to figure out if what I said was true. "What do you mean 'back to business'?"

"The front business to this means work that I can't fudge. You wouldn't understand. Demons have a different setup. Plus, it's not like you can't go back to Hell where you belong, and it's as nice as this dump. If I mess my dad's business up, then I'm fucked."

"You won't be fighting with us?" she asked. "Like I said, the demon council won't sit tight on this, especially if I can get that vampire out there—Did I hear his name correctly? Matt? — To testify regarding his knowledge. Once he does that and the rest of us report in. It will only be a matter of time before we can attack, and I'd like you to get the information on the Sayyaad. I'll pay you too."

"My help? Did you just forget that Victor wants me dead? I can't even stick a foot on coven ground without a swarm coming right at me."

"If we have others fighting alongside, wouldn't you be able to go looking for it?"

"Getting away would be impossible. I'll be fighting the whole time."

"I need this Sayyaad though."

"Why? I don't get the big hubbub. What's the real deal with finding this Sup?"

There was a long pause as she debated. I watched her every move. "I want to take down four members of the demon council."

"Now I'm intrigued." I arched a single brow. "Why?"

"They killed my father, little brother, and sister. Revenge is a dish best served cold. They think I am on their side, but I'm not, and if I can find this Sayyaad, I'll have a chance to avenge their deaths."

That was not the answer I expected. I didn't know the council had done anything to her family. If this was news to me, it made me wonder if Abraxas knew. I would need to ask him.

"Mandy... does Brax know about this?"

"No. I don't think so.... but I want to find out, and this is why I took one of his objects of power." The succubus held in tears with a half-smile. "You called me Mandy."

Maybe she wasn't as heartless as I'd thought. Still, she was untrustworthy *and* manipulative. I had to be cautious. I continued to observe her, but piped up quickly with an answer. "Yeah, old habits. You need to tell him."

"No, he sits on the council with them. I am not sure I can risk asking him. What if he is involved?"

"I think you have Abraxas pegged all wrong."

"Are you sure about that?"

"Absolutely. Do you have proof that he knew they murdered your family?"

"I don't, but he didn't believe my mother or me."

"Hmm, I wonder why."

"Because we're succubi. Our ability to persuade people is unmatched."

"You mean manipulate? I wouldn't trust you—I don't trust you. There are other reasons I won't work with you either. I don't want to guess the outcome of an otherwise straightforward job. It's never easy with you, is it?"

"Aaima, I can't apologize enough for what I said and did to you. My mom threatened to lock me up if I kept seeing you. I was terrified of her threats. She hated our monogamy. Hated that I let you in and couldn't use my powers on you. 'It's not natural,' she said. She told me I would be an outcast if I continued. I never stopped loving you."

"I'll talk to Brax about this. I am sure we can dig up some leads, but you're on your own for the coven thing, understand? Like I said, the information you want is in Victor's office. Send someone in while the rest of us fight."

"You're going? I thought you said you wouldn't."

"No, I said I wouldn't help you because the moment I go there, it's a battle, and I need to prepare my body and mind. Also, you better pay me if I find anything about the killing of your family. I don't work for free."

"Wow, you're not how I remember you."

"Nope. That happens when you collect supernatural bounties for a living. My mom died, and then my first love smashed my heart to pieces. Then I watched a monster kill my other parent before it came after me. Yet somehow, I survived. I'm jaded and don't want to deal with your manipulations."

"I... I didn't know."

"Now you do, and you might be telling the truth about your family, but your mom got a hold of you and twisted you right up. We always have a choice, Mammon. I can't say I'm the best at making them. I'm a little jacked up myself, but at least I chose the right thing and pulled myself back up. Luckily, I've made the right friends. What will you do?"

She went silent. I waited for her to speak. Her eyes locked with mine. I didn't understand why it was so hard to just look at her. I loved Abraxas. Yet the pain from the old wound boiled near the surface.

She had fucked up and left me to fend off several demons by myself. Mammon/Mandy had talked me into leaving Fenris at home that night too. What hurt the most is she knew her mother had sent them to kill me. My dad showed up right when I almost lost and helped me send them back into the depths of Hell. I cried for hours that night. We had been together for years before she betrayed me and left me to die.

"I want to make this right. My mother is dead to me, and I am doing what I want with my life. I want succubi to be seen differently." She bit her lip and gave me a once over.

"Well then, you strut right into that demon council of yours and get them to take down Victor's coven."

She licked her lips and nodded. "I will try."

"No, you will succeed. We're getting Abraxas in on this." I cracked open the office door and yelled out for him.

"Are you sure?" she asked.

"I'm sure. Trust me," I said. "You know you can. I've never betrayed your trust." It felt weird to say those words. I wasn't outright betraying her, but I certainly wasn't about to tell her what I was planning.

Chapter Twenty-Three

The Next Step

Aaima

Abraxas walked into the office with Matt. Braun stood at the front door. Mammon's eyes dimmed, and I could sense her personality change. She'd been putting on a show for them. Was it to appear stronger than them, or was it to hide her vulnerability? I couldn't decide.

"Mammon has something she needs to tell you," I said.

Brax folded his arms across his chest and glared in her direction. "Make it quick. This better be worth my time."

"The Four are responsible for the murders of my father and siblings." Mammon combed her long fingernails through her hair and straightened her tunic out before she took a stand and walked around.

"Do you have proof?" Brax's eyes followed her around the room with suspicion.

"Wait, who are the Four?" I had never asked about further details on the Infernal Council, so I was clueless about its members.

Mammon turned to Brax. "You've never told her about them? Why?"

"Because I didn't ask, and I wasn't interested." I said before he could answer.

"Precisely that reason." Brax added. "The Four are siblings and frankly, the worst our kind offers. They are brutal and powerful, and they hide their misdeeds well. No one has ever punished them for their crimes. I have long suspected they want to take over Hell. I am positive killing your father was on their list to achieve it."

"If you suspected, why didn't you do anything?" Mammon's voice trembled. "You, the one demon who remains neutral."

"I had no leads to follow and no proof. But back to my earlier question. Do you have evidence I can use against them? That's the only way we can get them." He cracked his neck and waited for her answer.

"I do. I will have it delivered to your club tonight, but you need to tell me under oath that you had nothing to do with my family's deaths." Mammon turned to Matt next. "And we need you, vampire," she said, poking his chest.

"What for?" Matt's eyebrow jerked up before he pushed her finger away.

Funny, it seemed most of those in the office had an aversion to her touch. It was eating at her every second that passed. I could hear it in her voice and see it in her eyes. It was subtle, but I knew the look well. Even all that time apart hadn't killed my memory.

"I want you to testify. We need a vampire that can tell

us everything. Tell them about Victor's plans. You won't be alone. The group of witnesses outside will be by your side."

"I don't know about that," Matt said, hesitating.

I chimed in. "We need this. It's the only way we'll have a chance at stopping your father."

Brax sighed. "Aaima's right. The other demons won't stand for this to go on. The council will have to decide. Either we fight with or without them. They hate looking bad, so I suspect they'll agree with the right persuasion tactics."

"That is where I come in," Mammon inserted.

Brax looked pissed, but nodded. "I'll take the oath now."

Mammon walked up to him and took a small knife out of the necklace around her neck. I stepped up and stood beside him, ready to pounce if she tried anything stupid.

"Blood to blood. Truth prevails. All lies undone," they said in unison.

"What the—" I was cut off when Brax extended his arm and pressed his finger against my lips.

"Blood to blood. Truth prevails. All lies undone. The truth

be revealed," they said again. Mammon cut her hand, then did the same to Brax's. They put their palms together and muttered in the true demon language. I couldn't make out what they said, but when they pulled away and held out their hands, a spark of gold flickered up from the wounds. The light grew, filling up the cuts before healing.

"What was that?" I grabbed Brax's hand, turning it over, inspecting it for anything that could be off.

"That was the confirmation I needed—He had nothing to do with the murders of my family."

"Of course I didn't," he said tersely.

"Well, shall we get going?" Mammon asked.

"Yes, we can call the council on the way and get the ball rolling," Brax said. "Braun, escort Mammon to my office. Matt will follow. I'll meet you all there."

"Yes, sir." Braun tried to direct everyone out the front door.

"I can escort myself, thank you very much." Mammon puffed.

"The council will convene in my office, so it needs to look

like we escorted you as a witness. Get with the damn program. Half your issues are always this. Undermining your colleagues makes them suspicious."

Brax made some brilliant points and pegged her down to a T. It seemed she hadn't really changed. Maybe she wanted to, but she was struggling to be her own person and didn't want to appear weak. I could believe her in seeking justice for her family's deaths, but the rest was dodgy at best.

Mammon asked Brax. "Why aren't you coming with us?"

"I need to make sure Aaima and the DBA are secure before leaving. I'll be right behind you."

"Hmm. Fine," were the only words that came out of her mouth, but she planted herself in the doorway.

"Get moving then... oh, and if I find out you have any ulterior motives, I'll take you down myself after we take care of the vampires." My gut told me to question her every action, no matter what. Mammon's intentions for her family might have been good, but she'd used the rest of us as pawns to get what she wanted.

"Is that all?" She glared at me.

"Yes, it is. I suggest you head out and do what needs to be done on your end and nothing else," I snapped back.

Braun coaxed her out the door with Matt a few steps ahead. Brax turned to me and cradled me in his arms.

"I am so glad you're okay. I had no idea what she'd do to you. If there is a demon you shouldn't put your trust in—it's her."

"Trust me. I know."

I watched the group of demons leave the parking lot before walking over and shutting the office door.

"I have something for you," I said.

"You got my amulet back?" he asked.

I walked back up to him and stood close. "Here." I pulled the amulet out of the confines of my shirt and held it out.

Brax's face paled. "How are you doing that? You shouldn't be able to wear it." His voice trailed off.

His face told me everything, just like Mammon's. Something about his amulet forbade others to wear it, but it sat comfortably around my neck, waiting for its owner to take it back.

"I have no idea how this is possible, but there it is around your neck." Brax reached over and cupped the amulet in his hand.

Gently, I removed his hand before taking it from around my neck. The chain was long, so I just looped it over the top of my head and held it one last time. "It knew my intentions."

"What do you mean, it knew?" he asked me.

"Your amulet has some sort of consciousness. Didn't you know?" Could he not feel it? It was like it was alive, filled with intelligence.

"What? No, I didn't. Now I am intrigued, but we still have the council mess to deal with." Brax couldn't tear his eyes away from his amulet. He lightly traced the old symbols on it with his index finger.

"I can't believe you got it back. Hey, where's Stefen?" He looked up and glanced around the office.

"Over here," Stef said, breaking his silence as his body appeared in the corner on the opposite side of us.

"We need you to get to Victor's office before Mammon." Brax continued to look at his amulet while he spoke.

"I can do that. I need to do this for you." Stef walked over right next to me.

"You can do this." I smiled warmly.

"I sure hope so, or we're screwed." He chewed his lip. His nerves were already setting in.

"You've gone there once already. You can do it again." I patted his shoulder and kept eye contact.

"But I stayed in ethereal form. I'll be coming out of it to grab the journal. Can I do that alone?" he asked.

I needed a moment to think. Yes, he could get there undetected, but what if Victor or the other vamps were in the office? What would Stef do next, and how well would he be able to fight?

Brax chimed in immediately. "I'll come with you," he said as he put the amulet around his neck.

"Won't that defeat the purpose of going in my true banshee

form?" Stef's eyebrow arched, and his face twisted up in confusion.

"I have my amulet back. I can tag along with you now, but here's the caveat: we have to stay connected somehow, so your form becomes mine and we're both invisible, or it won't work."

"What do you mean, stay connected? Physically touching? Or like a magical thread through a spell, because I don't know any and I am not sure Aaima does either. Do you?" Stef asked.

"No spells, just physically touching. So, we get to waltz by all those Bloodsuckers holding hands and they'll be none-the-wiser. Just don't let go."

I giggled. "You're telling me you're gonna hop, skip, and walk into Victor's mansion, holding Stef's hand to keep yourself invisible? Oh man, if only I could watch this happen."

Brax responded by rolling his eyes. "I am trying to make sure he makes it out unscathed. Do you want the vamps to tear him up?"

"Of course not! I just... the image in my head right now." I stifled back more laughter.

Stef chuckled under his breath. "It is a funny image, considering what we are stepping into."

"Exactly. Why so dang serious?" I tussled Brax's hair and gave him a peck on the cheek. "I know you got this. Thank you for wanting to protect him. This right here is one of the many reasons I love you."

Brax wrapped his arms around me. His gaze locked on mine. "Love you too. And... I'm sorry about earlier—with her."

"You don't need to apologize. Trust me, I get your anxiety and frustration. That she-devil is something else. She might help us in the fight against Victor, but I wouldn't trust her not to stab us in the back later."

"Let's keep a watchful eye on her then. So, what comes next?" Brax lightly kissed my forehead.

"I think it's time we get ready to go to Victor's. You go do your council business to ensure the demons are on our side. I'll gather the rest of our forces, and then we take out the big bad." I punched my fist into my open hand.

"Well, let's put the next steps in motion."

"Sounds good."

"See you soon." Stef waved and sat down on the couch.

I walked Brax to the door, watched him walk out to his car, then he drove off. When he was out of sight, I closed the door and sighed. "I hope this works, or we're all fucked."

Chapter Twenty-Four

What's Right. Not Easy.

Aaima

I paced back and forth from the door to my desk. Stef and Fenris keenly watching me. Waiting for me to say something more. This was hard. I was in charge. The thought sank in deep.

I am in charge now, like Dad... what would he do? I can't mess this up. Lives are at stake.

I had been confident until the moment I had time to reflect. Even the best-laid plans could end up going awry. I had to make sure ours were foolproof, but even then, there was no guarantee.

"Stef, I need to say this now. When we face off with Victor and his coven...." My voice trailed off.

He finished the sentence for me. "There's no coming back from it."

"Yeah. We have plans, but that doesn't mean they'll play out how we expect them to. Honestly, I am surprised that your first recon went so well. Perhaps too well? I might be too much in my head at this point now that the adrenaline's run out." Fenris came to my side and rubbed his head against my fidgeting arm.

Stef fidgeted with his glasses but inhaled and said, "I have to admit—same. We just need to go for it, I think. You have done so much for me in such a short time. This is the least I can do. Brax is a demon and has tricks up his sleeve. I'll be okay. I won't sit around and let things happen. My resolve is strong and I will fight." He lowered his eyes to the ground. "I will not stand there like I did when the beast took my mother."

"You're right. Brax accompanying you is our best bet. I'll just try to keep everyone else outside, but I bet Mammon will have a plan to get the information too."

"I'll get to it first, I promise."

"Don't make promises you can't keep," I said with a playful lilt, my eyes glinting mischievously, trying to lighten the mood.

"I'll get it first." Stef insisted with more seriousness to his tone.

Hopefully, we'd make it out without my secret getting into Mammon's hands. She might have loved me once, but I knew for a fact that she cared more about her vengeance. Even with her evidence being presented to the demon council, she'd still screw over anyone just to get the ending she wanted.

I thought about what Dad and Brax mentioned. The Sayyaads were the equalizers. I'd have to neutralize the situation if shit went sideways.

And in the Sup world, it tended to do just that.

I took Stef and Fenris down to the basement of the DBA the next day. Brax called, saying the situation turned volatile. One of the Four had killed a council member and took off. The other siblings followed.

He predicted it, but luckily, the remaining members were willing to help with the vampire situation before it became too much to handle. I was happy we managed to secure backup from them at all.

Matt slipped the warning notice to his inside contact. Those with him would wear his family crest on a bracelet around their wrists. They would turn to fight at the last minute—our surprise attack. I had David gather the DBA folks up. They were ready when we were.

I dug through the old trunks in the corner, brushing off layers of dust as I searched for any armor that might fit Stef's slender frame. "Come here, try this on," I called over my shoulder, hauling out a hardened leather chest covering.

He came over and I helped ease the stiff material over his t-shirt, adjusting the straps and buckles until it sat properly over his chest. "Hmmm, that will do," I muttered, grabbing a pair of worn leather wrist guards from the pile and handing them over for him to slide on.

"Shouldn't we spell some of our items first?" Stef asked, flexing his wrists experimentally in the guards.

"I don't know," I admitted with a sigh. "I'm not always the best with magic."

"But you have it in you," Stef encouraged. "Perhaps there's something in the new grimoire that could help?"

I considered it for a moment before shaking my head. "You're probably right, but I keep forgetting that resource is even there. It's still so new, and I hate feeling like I need the crutch, you know?"

Stef nodded, a smile of understanding crinkling his eyes. "Completely."

"Here," I said, grabbing the ancient book from the nightstand. "You scan through this and tell me what you find?"

I passed the weighty tome into his hands, hoping he could find the right spell to get us through this fight in one piece.

"Let's get Fenris ready." I opened a large leather chest with a wolf's head on it. Inside lay pieces of armor that Dad had left for Fenris. Until now, we never expected we'd need them, but I wasn't about to take the chance with so many vamps around and Fenris's body wide open for attack.

I looked at Fenris standing next to Stef. Something changed in him. He seemed larger than he was yesterday. Did he grow overnight? I know we've been busy, but how could I miss that? His huge yellow eyes locked on mine, and his lips curved up.

I kept thinking back to the part in Dad's old book mentioning how powerful the Sayyaad with her wolf could become. I wasn't even close.

Today, I craved that power. But that wasn't necessarily a good thing. I didn't want to turn out like Mammon. It always seemed like it was easy to give in and do the wrong thing. Doing the right thing was harder.

Dad always said, "*right didn't mean easy, but it meant you were being honest with yourself and others.*"

Maybe the real power was integrity. It was hard to fight anything if you weren't whole.

Chapter Twenty-Five

Let's Start a Fight

Aaima

We snuck up to the coven's compound with quite the menagerie in tow. Demons, humans, Sup-touched, and a few other stragglers who knew we were going up against Victor. I could see the massive mansion the vampires shared from the forest tree line. I studied the scene in front of me. Brax and Stefen were well on their way in, hidden from sight. They'd be entering from the backside through an entrance meant only for vamps. Thanks to Matt, we had a head start on Mammon.

I felt her presence behind me as she slithered up to me.

"You could always change your mind." She smiled coyly.

"Change my mind about what?" I glanced at her, unblinking.

"Abraxas. You should be with me." Mammon bit her lip while she took in the sight of me. I had to admit, she was a mild distraction with her advances, but I was done with all of it and had been for years.

"Never going to happen." The words rolled off my tongue with no emotion.

"You know what they say about never saying never."

I redirected her focus. "Concentrate on the fight to come. Are your people ready?"

"Yes. When did you become so stiff and serious?"

"The moment I lost my father."

She didn't utter a word to me after that. We kept our positions and eyes on the mansion. We waited in silence, our allies shifting around enough their legs didn't go numb. I welcomed it, but I could tell Mammon hated every second.

When the gate to the compound opened, I signaled to Braun, Matt, and David.

We charged forward, spreading out to launch a multi-pronged attack. Everything blurred into chaos after that initial clash. Vampires swarmed at us from all sides, trying to beat down our ranks with their superior numbers. But we held our ground, determined to see this through.

From my left I suddenly heard cries of alarm — Fenris had launched a surprise attack from the east side. He was a whirlwind of claws and fangs, flinging vampires into the air effortlessly and shredding them limb from limb. Their severed arms and legs littered the ground like macabre confetti. I offered a grim smile at the sight — the tide was turning.

I fought my way toward the main house, cutting down two lesser vampires in my path. Three guards stood ready to halt my advance. One directly in front, two more fanned out on either side. They meant to surround me. I could tell by the murderous glint in their crimson eyes that they knew exactly who I was.

"Ready to dance, boys?" I smirked, readying my weapon—dad's sword.

"Victor would have let you live if you left well enough alone," one of them muttered under their breath.

"Less talking, more fighting. I'm not one to chat." I swung the sword around and positioned myself to take out whichever one took a jab at me first.

"Come on, men rip that bitch's throat out," the one in front of me scowled.

I saw the whirlwind of black fur rush toward him. I smirked. "Time to die."

Fenris leaped into the air and latched onto the back of one vamp. I twirled around, slicing into the vamp on my left. The one to my right stood with his mouth gaping open and eyes wide.

"You're next!" I belted out before taking the blade down into his shoulder.

I shoved it in hard and then pulled it out. He looked up at

his dead comrades. "But, how? You moved with such speed?"

"I'm not normal, remember?" I said before I cut his head clean off.

Fenris pranced over, looking quite pleased with himself. A trail of headless vampires lay behind him. As we stood side by side, a sliver of calm surrounded us. I took in the scene ahead. Several more coven members headed toward us in a blood rage.

"Ready for the next bunch?" I asked.

"Sure am," he answered before we both jumped into action. One by one, we cut down any vamp who tried to stop us. I wanted to get to the back a quick as possible and make sure Brax and Stef got out. Then I heard the snarl of the beast that almost killed me.

Chapter Twenty-Six

Face Off with the Beast

Aaima

A chill reverberated down my spine. I could feel the heat of the beast's breath on the back of my neck. A sharp claw touched me below my shoulder blades. It dug into my flesh. I gritted my teeth. I should have known it wouldn't be that easy.

Whirling to face the creature who had taken my world away from me, I looked into its big red eyes and stood my ground. "So, we meet again."

A deep growl rumbled up from its chest. I raised my sword, ready to block an attack. But the beast sat down, right there, and continued to observe my every move.

Dark shadows seeped out from under its belly and curled around its long-furred body, shooting toward the sky. Fenris snarled and crept up to its right side. The beast turned its head and sniffed him, but did nothing else.

"Stef told us you're being controlled. That you might be innocent. Forced to do horrible things by a witch?" I continued to stare deep into its eyes.

It grunted as if to say *yes*, then nudged its head in Fenris's direction, who accepted and nudged back.

"We want to help, but we don't know how," I continued as the beast brushed my forehead.

I didn't want to lose eye contact with the creature, but knew that Brax and Stef would be out at any moment.

"I need to check on this door right here. I am going to turn around for just a minute."

The creature's head nodded up and down—Good, It understood. I turned and peeked around the side of the building. I just needed to see them before they took off into the wooded area behind the mansion.

I thought I'd catch a few vamps back there, but spotted none. Maybe they thought this creature would destroy anyone who came this way?

"Nothing to see back there, Fen. How long do I give them before I barge through that back door?" I said, turning back around.

"I don't know. I'll follow your lead. What about—" His slick nose pointed at the beast behind us.

"Does it have a name? Has it tried to communicate telepathically?"

"Sort of. He's scared, I know that."

"Hmm, imagine that..." My words trailed off as I took another look around the corner.

Muffled shouts come from inside. I held my sword at the ready. The door burst open and out flew Stef and Brax. They scrambled toward the tree line with three vamps close behind them.

I leaped into action. Two of the vamps had the beginnings of Bloodlust setting in. *Shit*. Thank Gods Matt gave us doses of the antidote.

My pulse kicked up. "Fenris, we need to take down the ones with signs of Bloodlust now!"

"Got it!"

"Take the one on the left." I charged forward and easily subdued my target. Fenris was just as quick. I made eye contact with Stef, who smiled and waved. I chuckled, waving back.

Brax grabbed hold of the last vampire left and Stef staked it in the heart before they cut its head off. I was impressed. I turned toward the door, but large, pale hands gripped my neck. A man that looked like an older version of Matt had me in his grasp.

"Meddling hunters never know when to leave things alone. Your father learned the hard way girl, and now I'm about to teach you the same lesson."

"Screw you," I gasped out.

He held on tight while my legs dangled in the air. His fingers pressed into my skin, making it harder to breathe. Then he tossed me.

I hit the pavement and rolled. It hurt like hell.

Before I could fully recover, he'd already walked over. Again, he picked me up but this time he slammed my body into the side of the mansion.

He leaned over me, his face hovering right above mine, sneering. I spat. The lump of saliva hit right below his left eye. He wiped it away with the back of his hand, then leaned in to sniff me. "Ah yes, you are like him, but... *different*. Unfortunately, I can't afford to let you live."

His dark eyes blazed with hatred as I struggled to get free. I brought my leg up and kicked him as hard as I could.

Fenris, Stef, and Brax were running up behind us.

"Don't be stupid! *Run*!" I yelled out.

"We're not leaving you," Stef blared back.

Victor glanced back at them. "Abraxas, I'd hate for this fight to continue. Retreat now and I'll forget this ever happened. Leave the others for us to handle and I'll reward you tenfold." His voice was unnervingly calm.

"Not a chance in Hell. I'm not taking your side."

"You picking a side instead of saving your own hide?" Victor laughed while he dug his sharp nails into the sides of my arms.

"Let her go now." Brax closed in on Victor's left side.

This vamp was tough. I knew the moment he grabbed me I was in for the fight of my life. I assumed it'd be up against the beast that killed my dad. Instead, it was against one of the oldest vampires in existence.

From the corner of my eye, I saw a whirl of black and red. Matt stood next to Victor. They glared at each other while Victor continued to pin me down.

"Father, stop this nonsense, please!" Matt reached out and gripped Victor's arm.

"Matthias, you have shamed me enough. If I have to, I will kill you myself."

"You'd kill your own son?" He appalled me.

"I must do what is good for the whole, not just the one. The vampires will rule over the humans and the Supernaturals will soon follow."

"There has to be a better way than this. You're infecting our kind and murdered someone who was your friend. This won't hurt just us, but it will endanger all Sups! Humans outnumber us!" Matt scoffed.

I hated this guy more by the minute. First, he killed my dad, then he sent a pack of rabid vamps after me on DBA property, on top of infecting his own people with Bloodlust, torturing creatures into submission to use them as weapons, and making witches do his bidding. But now he was ready to kill his own son. And for what? *For power*. The good of the vampires? How was any of this good? He'd gone mad.

I knew it was time to put my Sayyaad powers to work. Victor made the mistake of touching me. I just needed to focus. I closed my eyes and inhaled a deep breath. Matt tried to get Victor to let me go, but he slammed me back into the wall, his hand on my chest.

He used his free hand to hold Matt at bay. I took advantage of the moment and laced my fingers around his wrist, gripping tight. Victor turned and watched me with curiosity. "You won't escape girl. Your attempts will only result in failure."

I scowled and squeezed his arm tighter — my resolve to focus becoming stronger. Victor laughed and applied more pressure to my body. The strength he had in one arm alone was astounding. I had no idea how mine would match his.

Take in his abilities. I inhaled deeply. The surge hit me like a shock of electricity. I could see a violet glow emit from my fingertips. Fenris had a luminesce around him, too. I reached out to my wolf. *Fenris, can you hear me? Attack his legs after I take in his abilities.*

His response filled my mind. *Done.*

Fenris snarled and attacked Victor's backside. I twisted his arm until his wrist snapped and flung him aside. The strength coursing through was I felt nearly overpowering.

Victor cracked his neck. "I knew it. I knew the rumors were true!" Then he lunged forward, and I met him as an equal.

We fought back and forth, trying to subdue one another. Matt ordered the other vampires to stay out of it as they approached the scene. He said something in an old vampire language, and somehow, I knew it meant that leaders fight each other despite never hearing the word before. I was far from a leader, but they heeded Matt's words.

Victor tossed me to the ground. I got him back and threw him into the wall. I checked to see if the demons were approaching from the side where the beast fought. I didn't need them to see what was going on.

Luckily, the beast was fighting off all the groups. Then I saw a woman in a black cloak and crushed velvety green dress. The witch approached. I sensed her magical ability from where I stood, and it pulsed through the air, rippling through my body. Victor charged at me again. Our swords clanked together.

"What will you do now, Sayyaad? You're no match for my

witch." His lips curled up in a sinister sneer before he bared his fangs and fanned out his arms in a show of power.

If the situation wasn't complicated enough, this made it worse. Matt was pushing Stefen and Brax back.

I ran toward them, yelling, "Get them out of here!"

Matt acknowledged and grabbed Stef's arm, taking him towards the trees, but he resisted and vanished, transforming into his ethereal form instantly. Brax remained at Matt's side. There was nothing I could do or say to make them go. I glanced around, taking in the scene. We needed the creature to let the demons through. The witch had to be taken down.

Fenris was aware of what I was thinking. Victor tried to grab me again, and I rolled out of the way. Fen was next to Brax, and I had to trust he'd share my thoughts with him and get the beast to let our allies join us before the witch unleashed her magic. But it was too late.

Chapter Twenty-Seven

The Vampire, the Witch, and the Long Road Ahead

Aaima

I had seconds to act. Victor needed to be subdued, though I doubted I could kill him. Matt must have known what I was thinking because he came charging for us while I pinned Victor to the ground. It took everything in me to keep him there.

"I should kill you right now while time allows," Matt told his father.

"Then do it... boy!" Victor snarled, challenging his own son in a mocking tone.

Matt needed to do this. While it was my job to keep the balance, I needed his help.

"If you have to, do it," I breathed out.

The look on Matt's face said it all - he was conflicted about what to do next. After all, this was his dad.

I could see the pain in my friend's face. If he let his father live, there would be more fighting and a risk of the Unsups finding out about us.

He must have realized as much because he winced, then grabbed my sword, and sliced his Victor's head off. Matt turned away, and the rest of the vamps stopped fighting.

A loud, shrill scream filled the air as the witch ran to the coven leader's body.

"My love! You killed your own father? How could you?" Tears streamed down her face. Shadows gathered around the bottom of her legs and her eyes filled with rage. She muttered a spell, throwing out immense power and knocking us all down to the ground.

She headed straight for Matt, so I did the only thing I could. I got up, rushed to his side, and stood in front of him.

The witch whistled, and the beast was by her side in seconds, pain flashing in its eyes. I could sense it now—the beast was trying to tell me something.

"Tear the Sayyaad to shreds, then kill Matt!" she screeched. When the beast stood still and didn't move on her command, she whirled on it, screaming, "Kill her now!"

It resisted her before she forced her magic on it again.

"Matt, get out of her sights! Go!" I ushered him away.

Fenris came to my aid. The witch and the beast struggled against each other's wills, but she won out and the beast tried to lash out. I still had some of Victor's vamp strength and speed, and used it to roll out of the way.

The beast rumbled toward me. Then Fenris and the beast twitched their ears, tossing their heads about. The Bloodlust vamps seemed to be affected, too.

Stef had unleashed his banshee scream. It was a muffled

sound that barely resonated in my ears, drowned out by my blood roaring through my veins. I was glad he was stubborn and stayed behind.

The witch tried to force her magic on the beast once more, but Stef's power was too strong.

It gave me the perfect opportunity to make my move. I stepped in between her and the beast.

Her magic hit me. But I was ready for it. I pulled on my Sayyaad powers from deep within and sent her spell rebounding back to her. She screamed as it struck, sending her toppling onto her back.

The demons took on the vamps who tried to fight Matt. It was strange that they still fought for Victor—he was dead and not coming back. They must have truly believed in his sickening cause.

I stood over the witch, ready to take her down, but she uttered some words and took out a small dagger strapped to her side. Before I could move to stop her, she sunk the blade into her own chest. Thick blood oozed from the wound and stained her mouth. and rasped out, “Victor, my love...”she gurgled right before her body went stiff.

“What the hell?” I asked at last.

In an instant, Matt was by my side. “That was unexpected. Tanith was devoted to my father, but killing herself? I never imagined.”

“I am the leader of this coven now!” he shouted. “Continue to fight my allies and we will take you all down. Or stop and know that the coven will be strengthened with me in charge.”

Mammon came running up with her forces, fighting off more vampires that remained around us. “Is it over?” she asked.

A dark reddish cloud sprung forth from the dead witch and knocked us down to the ground. Every single demon, vampire, and human screamed out in agony. It burned like thousands of red-hot needles as it tore through every inch of my body. I bit down on my lip and held my pain in.

The beast came to me and gently nipped my arm. I sat up and shook off whatever the witch's power had done to us, looking around to see the damage that her last-ditch effort for her dead lover caused.

Most of the lower demons were completely immobilized. Even Brax and Mammon struggled to get up. She had to have been one of the most powerful witches I would ever encounter. And she wasted her magic on a radical vampire's dream of domination over the world.

Mammon sat up. "What was that?"

"Powerful magic," I muttered before I got to my feet. I put my hand out and helped her up. "Did you find it?"

"Find what? Oh, the lead to the Sayyaad? No, someone had removed the information from Victor's office when I got there. Probably a vamp loyal to him. He no doubt wanted the Sayyaad for himself to gain more power. I will search later, but for now, the demons will return to our homes."

She sighed. "I'll visit you sometime later. I'm not done trying. You'll be mine again. I just know it." Then she planted a kiss on my cheek and left just as Stef and Brax walked up to me.

"What was that about?" Brax asked.

I scoffed, "She thinks she's going to get me back."

"Oh." He took hold of my hand in an adorably possessive manner.

David and the DBA crew gathered around.

"Thanks everyone. This was one tough fight," I said loudly.

"Let's get the hell out of here and head to John's cabin," David added.

"Hunter's stew all around!" Everyone cheered in unison.

"Oh, did John offer?" I asked David.

"Yes, he says you should come back with us too."

"I'll be there shortly. You guys head out first. I'm right behind you. I just need to tie up all the loose ends."

David gave his signature swift nod, and the DBA crew sprang into action. Boots stomped across the concrete floor as they grabbed their gear and headed out. As they passed by, a few of the guys clapped me on the back, the heavy thuds jarring me out of my daze. 'Nice work back there kid, just like your old man,' they bellowed over the chaos. I felt my cheeks flush and gave an awkward half-smile, half-nod as I mumbled thanks, not used to the praise. The ruckus faded as the last of them exited, leaving me standing there feeling a complicated mix of pride and humility at being compared to my father. Matt was conversing with several of his own. He stopped and stepped forward to face the crowd. "I think we can call it a day. I'm in charge of the Sanguine Coven from now on." He hugged me, whispering, "Thank you."

Fenris was lying next to the beast with Stef sitting beside them.

"Well guys, this is it. Let's head out."

Fenris, Stef, and Brax all came to my side. We walked back toward the entrance of the compound, and I turned to face the beast.

"That means you too," I said.

He got up and followed.

"Where are we headed?" Stef asked me.

"John's cabin for right now," I answered.

"And after that? What about the creature?"

"I think he's with us now, but there's a long road ahead. Something in my gut says this isn't quite over yet."

Chapter Twenty-Eight

What Comes Next

Aaima

We got back to the truck. The beast was big. There was only one place he'd fit, so he hopped in the truck's bed. I had no idea what I was going to do with him and Fenris. We determined it was a male. Still no name though, but we'd get there.

"What if we moved the headquarters to my old house? It's right at the edge of the city. We could keep an eye out on the creature; learn more about it." Stef suggested, as we got into the cab.

"Hmm. What about your mom? We know she escaped. Would she be okay with this?"

"I have bad news." He grimaced slightly. "I found some papers when I removed the information Victor had on you from his office. They've done something to her that can't be reversed... I don't think I'll be seeing her again." The inner edge of his eyelids filled with tears. He cleared his throat and held them back.

"Stef." I reached out and touched his arm. "I'm sorry, friend. We didn't need to lose her too. Maybe we can figure out how to get her back? Banshees can't die, can they?"

"I honestly have no idea, but Mom had a massive library. Maybe we can find some answers there. She left the estate to me."

"Okay, we'll talk about this more another time. Let's get to John's, eat, and then go from there."

When we made it to John's, the camp fires were already blazing, and all around, tables filled with hunters who were eating and talking.

So many people I had grown up with over the years had come out to help me. Several approached us and patted me on the back.

"We're glad you're in charge. You got the makings of a true leader. Keep it up."

It was crazy to hear the words over and over from different hunters. It also made me feel like I had finally found my way.

I walked around and thanked everyone for their help. I looked for David next, but then John came out of his cabin and I rushed into his arms.

"You did it. I'm so proud. I had to finish the rites to make sure that Wendigo didn't come back alive. Sorry I couldn't be there." He roughed up my hair with his hand.

"The whole crew had my back, and you had it elsewhere, thank you." I smiled and squeezed him tighter.

"Oh, that's some hug." He chuckled.

"If anyone comes close to being a dad, it's you, John, and you know it."

"Your dad said the same once. I wish he was here."

"Me too." I agreed.

"Well, what's next? I see that beast lingering near the edge of the trees."

"I want to keep him. There's a weird bond between us and Fenris—I gotta figure it out. I can sense its thoughts, and our connection keeps getting stronger. Fen doesn't seem to mind the extra company either."

"Hmm." He scratched at his chin in thought. "Keeping the beast that killed your father, that's something. We'll figure it out. Hopefully, it's something good for a change.

"Yeah. Agreed."

I sat down in one chair on the porch, and John followed me.

"I think I'm going to move the DBA to Stef's mansion. More room for large critters and a place no one is familiar with."

"Well, that's an idea. Are you sure?" He asked.

"Yes. Stefen's mom collected a large library on the supernatural world. I think I can help him figure out what happened to his mom and find out more about myself too. Plus, I feel like a fresh start."

"Do what you need to do." He smiled.

"I'll have David move into Dad's old office. He deserves it," I piped up.

David swung his head around, his eyes big. "What did I just hear?" he asked.

"You're leveling up in the company."

"Oh yeah? Oh dear. I'll take it! Thank you for trusting me."

"Enough talk about business. We need a solid break! Let's drink!" I stood up and went over to the cooler and grabbed a beer. I cracked it open and chugged half of it. If anything, I deserved *one* beer after the shit we went through.

Everyone cheered. I watched the fire dance with Abraxas's arms wrapped around me. In the pit of my stomach, I knew something more would happen.

It excited part of me — the possibilities, but another part was anxious about the potential complications.

"Once we're done blowing off steam, let's head to Stef's house. We'll check the entire property and clear out anything we need to. Then we will be ready to use the new place for the work ahead."

"Really? You want to move DBA headquarters there?" He grinned ear to ear.

"Yes. I like it. You'll get your home back and there's ample room for the beast and Fenris. But I have the feeling another fight is coming. We need the space for training and, like you said, your mom has a massive library at our disposal. I'd be stupid to reject your offer."

"I'm ready, we've got this," He said.

"We *are* ready." Brax's face filled with determination.

"Yeah. I guess we are," I sighed, uncertainty still plaguing my thoughts. "Let's take some time to recharge and get our heads straight before diving in."

"That, we can all agree on," Stef said through a yawn. We all relaxed around the fire. Enjoying the company around us. Yet...

The nervous feeling in my gut intensified. This wasn't the end, only the beginning. A beginning to what, I didn't know, but we'd soon find out.

To be continued.

ACKNOWLEDGEMENTS

This one is hard to write as there are many people out there who have helped me along the way. A big thank you to my husband for believing in me and helping me get this book finished. Another thank you to Ali for everything you've done. A big shout out to Jamie, Trish, and Kitty. I know I am not always as in touch as other friends, so I appreciate your friendship and willingness to help me along my author journey when I finally poke my head out of my cave. A thank you to my sister Skye and all the help she's provided. Thank you's to Inessa for edits, Emrhett for the chapter headers, and if I have forgotten someone just know I am immensely grateful. And thank you to the readers who pick this book up and give a new author a chance. I am glad you are here.

DEAREST READER,

You've made it to the end of the story. I look forward to sharing further installments later as there is much more to tell! If you enjoyed this book, please consider leaving Bounty a review. Every review helps authors get their books to more readers. All Because of You, yes you. Each review matters! I'll take them all from one to five stars. Feedback is invaluable. I also encourage you to subscribe to my bi-monthly newsletter so I can get to know you. If you sign up you'll get writing updates, sneak peeks, character arts, and special newsletter only giveaways plus MORE. CLICK to join my list today. Reading this book in physical form? Flip to *About the Author* and find my linkt.ree QR code.

You can also find me on Instagram, Facebook, and sometimes TikTok. I also love Pinterest and look forward to connecting further.

About the Author

"Where the dark meets the light & Monsters, myths, and fairytales collide.

Alexis (otherwise known as Adalynd to some) is a wife, mother, author, and designer. Alexis writes Dark YA and Cozy Fantasies when she's not parading around as her other author ego Adalynd (who needs grit and spice).

Hoarder of craft supplies, coffee cups, yarn, bandanas, and books. ***A*** loves tacos, tea, and toast (with cinnamon & sugar). When she's not momming, she's writing, creating, gardening,

DIYing, and for sure playing her favorite video game Fallout. She's pretty introverted, but can be coaxed out of her cave with the promise of good conversation and tasty food.

She also enjoys spending time with her family and has been married to the love of her life for fifteen plus years.

A currently lives in the majestic state of Arizona (her homeland) where she keeps her eye out for spicy spiders (scorpions), has a growing petting zoo that includes chickens, ducks, cats, dogs, salamander, a red bearded dragon, mini horse, and one cute white rabbit too.

She hopes you'll take a walk in the forest of her imagination and join her as she wanders through her worlds and stories.

Connect with Adalynd online.

The Super Secret Page

Want extras, giveaways, and news from Adalynd's desk? Subscribe to her newsletter to get access to her super secret page that has chapter sneak peeks of future releases, character art, and more.

Grayves Garden

Books by Adalynd

Other Works by Adalynd Grayves:

Given to the Wolf King

Dark Souls

Calypso's Song

www.ingramcontent.com/pod-product-compliance
Lightning Source LLC
Chambersburg PA
CBHW070551310726
48982CB00011B/1540/J

* 9 7 9 8 9 8 8 9 5 4 0 0 2 *